"May I be so optimistic as to assume you're on your way back to Athens?"

She batted overly innocent lashes at him while smiling sweetly.

"I arrived last night for as long as it takes."

His Adonis mask remained impassive. The man was an absolute robot—if robots came in worn denim and snug T-shirts that strained across sculpted shoulders, with blond hair so closely cropped it gleamed like a golden helmet.

"As long as it takes to what?" she asked, and started again for the kitchen, tingling with uneasy premonition as she scoffed, "Throw me out?"

"See? I knew you weren't stupid."

Dani Collins discovered romance novels in high school and immediately wondered how a person trained and qualified for *that* amazing job. She married her high school sweetheart, which was a start, and then spent two decades trying to find her fit in the wide world of romance-writing—always coming back to Mills & Boon® Modern™.

Two children later, and with the first entering high school, she was placed in Harlequin's Instant Seduction contest. It was the beginning of a fabulous journey towards finally getting that dream job.

When she's not in her 'Fortress of Literature', as her family calls her writing office, she works, chauffeurs children to extra-curricular activities, and gardens with more optimism than skill. Dani can be reached through her website at www.danicollins.com

This is Dani's sizzling sexy debut for Mills & Boon® Modern™ Romance!

NO LONGER FORBIDDEN?

BY
DANI COLLINS

MILLS & BOON

First published in Great Britain 2013
by Mills & Boon, an imprint of Harlequin (UK) Limited.
Harlequin (UK) Limited, Eton House, 18-24 Paradise Road,
Richmond, Surrey TW9 1SR

© Dani Collins 2013

ISBN: 978 0 263 89972 6

Harlequin (UK) policy is to use papers that are natural, renewable and recyclable products and made from wood grown in sustainable forests. The logging and manufacturing process conform to the legal environmental regulations of the country of origin.

Printed and bound in Spain
by Blackprint CPI, Barcelona

NO LONGER FORBIDDEN?

I've drafted this first book dedication in my head a thousand times, but the one consistent has always been: For Doug.

There are other treasured people I must thank for their encouragement: my awesome parents, my adored sisters and their terrific spouses, my supportive in-laws, and my cousin who wants me to become famous so she can brag about a connection to someone other than those A-listers she already has.

I have to thank my children, of course, for only interrupting my writing time for blood or flood. I especially have to thank them for finding, when they were very little, a way to let me write. They made friends with the most amazing children who possessed the most amazing parents. I very much have to thank their Other Moms and their families for embracing mine.

CHAPTER ONE

NICODEMUS MARCUSSEN rose to shake hands with his lawyer, his muscles aching with tension as he kept his reaction to all they'd discussed very much to himself.

"I know this is a difficult topic," his lawyer tried.

Nic shook off the empathy with a cool blink and a private, *No, you don't*. Nic trusted Sebastyen, but only within the framework of the media conglomerate Nic had fought to run after Olief Marcussen's disappearance. Sebastyen had been one of Nic's first supporters, believing in Nic's leadership skills despite his inexperience. Nic was grateful, but they weren't friends. Nic eschewed close relationships of every kind.

"I appreciate your advice," Nic said with aloof sincerity. Everything Sebastyen had presented was the height of practicality, outweighing any sentiment that might have held Nic back. "It's definitely time to consider it as the anniversary approaches. I'll let you know how I'd like to proceed," he concluded in dismissal.

Sebastyen hovered, appearing to want to add something, but Nic glanced at his watch. His days were busy enough without social chit-chat.

"I only wanted to reiterate that it would be helpful if both next of kin agreed," Sebastyen blurted.

"I understand," Nic drawled, keeping his patronizing

tone muted but heard. It was enough of a butt-out to have
the lawyer nodding apologetically and making haste to
leave. Nic was quite sure the entire corporation, along with
the rest of the world, followed the escapades of the *other*
next of kin, but he wouldn't abide open speculation about
how he'd gain her cooperation.

The fact was, he already had an idea how he'd accomplish it. He'd been putting things together in his mind even
as Sebastyen had been stating his case.

As Sebastyen closed the office door Nic went back to
his desk and the courier envelope he'd received that morning. Bills of every description came out by the handful,
their disarray as fluttery and frivolous as the woman who'd
racked them up. The forget-me-not-blue notepaper was a
particularly incongruous touch. He reread the swooping
script.

Nic,
My bank cards aren't working. Kindly sort it out and
send the new ones to Rosedale. I'm moving in this
weekend for some downtime.
Ro.

His initial reaction had been, *downtime from what*? But
for once Rowan's self-serving behavior was a convenience
to him. Since she hadn't got the message when he'd stopped
her credit cards two months ago, he'd confront her and do
what Olief should have done years ago. Make her grow up
and act responsibly for a change.

Rosedale.

A warm sense of homecoming suffused Rowan O'Brien
as she climbed the hill and looked over the sprawling vineyard surrounding the sturdy house of gray stone and mul-

lioned windows. The turreted Old English mansion was out of place against the white beach and turquoise water, pure folly on a Mediterranean island where white stone columns and flowing architecture typically reigned, but it had been built to indulge a loved one so Rowan adored it with all her heart. And here she was free.

She'd sent the taxi ahead with her things, initially frustrated that her finances had stalled to the point where she'd had to take the ferry from the mainland, but the slow boat had turned out to be therapeutic. As much as she'd ached to see the house again, she had needed the time to brace herself for its emptiness.

With a bittersweet throb in her chest she descended to the lawn, ignored her luggage on the stoop and tried the door, half expecting it to be locked and wondering where she'd put her key. She'd left a message for the housekeeper, but wasn't sure Anna had received it. Rowan's mobile had stopped working along with everything else. Very frustrating.

The door was unlocked. Rowan stepped into silence and released a sigh. She had longed to come for ages but hadn't been able to face it, too aware that the heart of the home was missing. Except…

A muted beat sounded above her. Footsteps crossed the second floor to the top of the stairs. Male, heavy steps…

Before she could leap to the crazy conclusion that by some miracle her mother and stepfather had survived, and were here after all, the owner of the feet descended the stairs and came into view.

Oh.

She told herself her reaction stemmed from the unexpectedness of seeing him face-to-face after so long, but it was more than that. Nic always made her heart trip and her breath catch. And—and this was new, since she'd thrown

herself at him in a hideous moment of desperation nearly
two years ago—made her die a little of abject mortification.

She hid that, but couldn't help reacting to his presence.
He was so gorgeous! Which shouldn't matter. She knew
lots of good-looking men. Perhaps none combined the
blond Viking warrior with the cold Spartan soldier quite
the way he did, but marble-carved jaws and chilly, piercing blue eyes were a mainstay among her mother's film
and stage crowd.

Nic's looks were the least of his attributes, though. He
was a man of unadulterated power, physically honed and
confident to the point of radiating couched aggression. Nic
had always been sure of himself, but now the authority he
projected was ramped to new heights. Rowan felt it as a
force that leapt from him to catch hold of her like a tractor
beam that wanted to draw her under its control.

Reflexively she resisted. There was no room for quiet
defensiveness when she came up against this man's aura.
She instinctively feared she'd drown if she buckled to his
will, so she leapt straight to a stance of opposition. Besides,
he was one of the few people she could defy without con-
sequence. She'd never had anything to lose with Nic. Not
even his affection. He'd hated her from day one—something that had always stung badly enough without him
proving it on her twentieth birthday by reacting to her kiss
with such contempt. She tried very hard not to care that
he didn't like her. She definitely didn't let herself show
how much it hurt.

"What a lovely surprise," she said, in the husky Irish
lilt that had made her mother famous, flashing the smile
that usually knocked men off their guard. "Hello, Nic."

Her greeting bounced off the armor of his indifference.
"Rowan."

She felt his stern voice like the strop of a cat's tongue—rough, yet sensual, and strangely compelling. It was a challenge to appear as unmoved as he was.

"If you left a message I didn't get it. My mobile isn't working." She hooked the strap of her empty purse on the stairpost next to him.

"Why's that, do you suppose?" he asked without moving, his eyes hooded as he looked down on her.

His accent always disconcerted her. It was as worldly as he was. Vaguely American, with a hint of British boarding school, and colored by the time he'd spent in Greece and the Middle East.

"I have no idea." Needing distance from the inherent challenge in his tone, she slipped out of her light jacket and moved into the lounge to toss the faded denim over the back of a sofa. Her boots clipped on the tiles with a hollow echo, sending a renewed pang of emptiness through her.

It struck her that Nic might be here for the same reason she'd come. She glanced back, searching for homesickness in his carved features, but his face remained impassive. He folded his arms, bunching his muscles into a stance of superior arrogance.

"No, I don't expect you do," he remarked with dry disparagement.

"I don't what?" she asked absently, still hopeful for a sign of humanity in him. But there was nothing. Disappointment poked at her with an itch of irritation. Sometimes she wished… *Stop it*. Nic was never going to warm up to her. She had to get over it. Get over *him*.

But how? she wondered, restlessly tugging away the elastic that had kept her hair from blowing off her head on the ferry. She gave her scalp a rub, rejuvenating the dark waves while trying to erase her tingling awareness of Nic.

"Your mobile stopped working along with your cards," he said, "but the obvious reason hasn't occurred to you?"

"That everything expired at the same time? It occurred to me, but that doesn't seem likely. They've always managed to renew themselves before." She used her fingers to comb her hair back from her face, glancing up in time to see his gaze rise from an unabashed appraisal of her figure.

Her pulse kicked in shock. And treacherous delight. The wayward adolescent hormones that had propelled her to the most singularly humiliating experience of her life were alive and well, responding involuntarily to Nic's unrelenting masculine appeal. It was aggravating that it took only one little peek from him to ramp her into a fervor, but she was secretly thrilled.

To hide her confusing reaction she challenged him, a vaguely smug smile on her face. It wasn't easy to stare into his eyes and let him know she knew exactly where his attention had been. She'd been drilled from an early age to make the most of her looks. She knew she appealed to men, but she'd never caught a hint of appealing to this one. What an intriguing shift of power, she thought, even as their eye contact had the effect of making her feel as though she stood at a great height, dizzy, and at risk of a long fall.

Deep down, she knew she was kidding herself if she thought she had *any* power over him, but she let herself believe it long enough to take a few incautious steps toward him. She cocked her hip, aware that her boot heels would make the pose oh-so-provocative.

"You didn't have to come all this way to bring me new cards, Nic. You seem like a busy man. What happened? Decided you needed a bit of family time?" Again she searched for a dent in his composure, some sign that he craved human contact the way lesser mortals like she did.

His iceman demeanor chilled several degrees and she

could almost hear his thoughts. Her mother might have been his father's lover for nearly a decade, but he'd never once thought of Ro as *family*.

"I am busy," he informed her, with his patented complete lack of warmth.

She'd never seen him show affection to anyone, so she ought not to let his enmity bother her, but he always seemed extra frosty toward her.

"I *work*, you see. Something you wouldn't know anything about."

For real? She shifted her weight to the opposite hip, perversely pleased that she'd snared his attention again, even though his austere evaluation was not exactly rich with admiration of her lean limbs in snug designer denim. He just looked annoyed.

Fine. So was she. "These legs have been dancing since I was four. I know what work is," she said pointedly.

"Hardly what I'd call earning a living, when all your performances involve trading on your mother's name rather than any real talent of your own. Next you'll tell me the appearance fee you get for clubbing is an honest wage. I'm not talking about prostituting yourself for mad money, Rowan. I'm saying you've never held a real job and supported yourself."

He knew about the club? Of course he did. The paparazzi had gone crazy—which was the point. She'd hated herself for resorting to it, very aware of how bad it looked while her mother was still missing, but her bank account had bottomed out and she'd had no other choice. It wasn't as if she'd spent the money on herself, although she wasn't in a mood to air *that* dirty little secret. Olief had understood that she had an obligation toward her father, but she had a strong feeling Mr. Judgmental wouldn't. Better to fight Nic on the front she could win.

"Are you really criticizing me for trading on my mother's name when you're the boss's son?"

He didn't even know how wrong he was about her mother's reputation. Cassandra O'Brien had pushed Rowan onto the stage because she hadn't been getting any work herself. Her reputation as a volatile diva with a taste for married men had been a hindrance to everyone.

"My situation is different," Nic asserted.

"Of course it is. You're always in the right, no matter what, and I'm wrong. You're smart. I'm stupid."

"I didn't say that. I only meant that Olief never promoted me through nepotism."

"And yet the superiority still comes across! But whatever, Nic. Let's take your condescension as read and move on. I didn't come here to fight with you. I didn't expect to see you at all. I was after some alone time," she added in a mutter, looking toward the kitchen. "I'm dying for tea. Shall I ask Anna to make for two, or…?"

"Anna isn't here. She's taken another job."

"Oh. *Oh*," Rowan repeated, pausing three steps toward the kitchen. Renewed loss cut through her. Anna's moving on sounded so…final. "Well, I can manage a cuppa. Do you want one, or may I be so optimistic as to assume you're on your way back to Athens?" She batted overly innocent lashes at him while smiling sweetly.

"I arrived last night to stay for as long as it takes."

His Adonis mask remained impassive. The man was an absolute robot—if robots came in worn denim and snug T-shirts that strained across sculpted shoulders and cropped their blond hair so closely it gleamed like a golden helmet.

"As long as it takes to what?" she asked as she started again for the kitchen, tingling with uneasy premonition as she scoffed, "Throw me out?"

"See? I knew you weren't stupid."

CHAPTER TWO

ROWAN swung back fast enough to make her hair lift in a cloud of brunette waves. She was so flabbergasted Nic might have laughed if he hadn't been so deadly serious.

"*You* stopped all my credit cards. And closed my mobile account. You did it!"

"Bravo again," he drawled.

"What a horrible thing to do! Why didn't you at least warn me?"

Outrage flushed her alabaster skin, its glow sexy and righteous. A purely male reaction of lust pierced his groin. It was a common enough occurrence around her and he was quickly able to ignore it, focusing instead on her misplaced indignance. A shred of conscience niggled that he hadn't tried to call her, but when dealing with a woman as spoiled as she was reasoning wasn't the best course. She was too sure of her claim. Far better to present a fait accompli. *She* had.

"Why didn't you tell me you'd dropped out of school?" he countered.

If she experienced a moment of culpability she hid it behind the haughty tilt of her chin. "It was none of your business."

"Neither are your lingerie purchases, but they keep arriving on my desk."

A blush of discomfiture hit her cheeks, surprising him. He hadn't thought her capable of modesty.

"This is so like you!" Rowan charged. "Heaven forbid you *speak* to me. Seriously, Nic. Why didn't you call to discuss this?"

"There's nothing to discuss. Your agreement with Olief was that he would support you while you were at school. You chose to quit, so the expense fund has closed. It's time to take responsibility for yourself."

Her eyes narrowed in suspicion. "You're enjoying this, aren't you? You've always hated me and you're jumping on this chance to punish me."

"*Punish* you?" The words *hate* and *stupid* danced in his head, grating with unexpected strength. He pushed aside an uncomfortable pinch of compunction. "You're confusing hate with an inability to be manipulated," he asserted. "You can't twine me around your finger like you did Olief. He would have let you talk him round to underwriting your social life. I won't."

"Because you're determined my style of life should be below yours? Why?"

Her conceit, so unapologetic, made him crack a laugh. "You really think you can play the equality card here?"

"You're his son; he was like a father to me."

Her attempt to sound reasonable came across as patronizing. Entitled. And how many times had he buckled to that attitude, too unsure of his place in Olief's life? He'd adopted the man's name, but only because he'd wanted to be rid of the one stuck on him at birth. In the end Olief had treated Nic as an equal and a respected colleague, but Nic would never forget that Olief hadn't wanted his son. He'd been ashamed he'd ever created him.

Then, when Nic had finally been let into Olief's life, this girl and her mother had installed themselves like an obstacle course that had to be navigated in order to get near him. Nic was a patient man. He'd waited and waited for Olief to set aside time for him, induct him into the fold. *Acknowledge* him. But it had never happened.

Yet Rowan thought she had a daddy in the man whose blood made Olief Nic's father. And when it had come down to choosing between them two years ago, Nic recalled with a rush of angry bile, Olief had chosen to protect Rowan and disparage Nic. Nic would never forgive her setting him up for *that* disgrace.

"You're the daughter of his mistress." How Olief could want another man's whelp mothered by his mistress but not his own child had always escaped Nic. "He only took you on because the two of you came as a package," Nic spelled out. He'd never been this blunt before, but old bitterness stewed with fresh antagonism and the only person who had kept him from speaking his mind all these years was absent. "You're nothing to him."

"They were lovers!"

Her Irish temper stoked unwilling excitement in him. With her fury directed toward him, he felt his response flare stronger than ever before. He didn't want to feel the catch. She was off-limits. Always had been—even before Olief had warned him off. Too young. Too wrong for him. Too expressive and spoiled.

This was why Nic hated her. He hated himself for reacting this way. She pulled too easily on his emotions so he wanted her removed from his life. He wanted this confused wanting to stop.

"They weren't married," he stated coldly. "You're not his relation. You and your mother were a pair of hangers-on. That's over now."

"Where do you get off, saying something like that?" she

demanded, storming toward him like a rip curl that wanted to engulf him in its maelstrom of wild passion.

He automatically braced against being torn off his moorings.

"How would you justify that to Olief?"

"I don't have to. He's dead."

His flat words shocked both of them. Despite his discussion with Sebastyen, Nic hadn't said the obvious out loud, and now he heard it echo through the empty house with ominous finality. His heart instantly became weighted and compressed.

Rowan's flush of anger drained away, leaving her dewy lips pale and the rest of her complexion dimming to gray. She was close enough that he felt the change in her crackling energy as her fury grounded out and despondency rolled in.

"You've heard something," she said in a distressed whisper, the hope underlying the words threadbare and desperate.

He felt like a brute then. He'd convinced himself that the disappearance hadn't meant that much to her. She was nightclubbing in their absence, for God's sake. But her immediate sorrow now gave him the first inkling that she wasn't quite as superficial as he wanted to believe. That quick descent into vulnerability made something in him want to reach out to her, even though they weren't familiar that way. The one time he'd held her—

That thought fuelled his unwanted incendiary emotions so he shoved it firmly from his mind. He was having enough trouble hanging on to control as it was.

"No," he forced out, trying to work out why he'd been able to hold it together in front of Sebastyen, who was closer to him than anyone, but struggled in front of Rowan. He feared she would see too deeply into him at a time when his defenses were disintegrating like a sandcastle under the tide. He couldn't look into her eyes. They were too anxious and demanding.

"No, there's been no news. But it'll be a year in two weeks. It's time to quit fooling ourselves they could have survived. The lawyers are advising we petition the courts to—" He had to clear his throat. "Declare them dead."

Silence.

When he looked for her reaction he found a glare of condemnation so hot it gave him radiation blisters.

With a sudden re-ignition of her temper, she spat, "You have the nerve to call *me* a freeloader, you sanctimonious bastard? Who benefits from declaring them dead? *You*, Nic. No. I won't allow it."

She was smart to fling away from him then, slamming through the door into the kitchen and letting it slap back on its hinges. Smart to walk away. Because that insult demanded retaliation, and he needed a minute to rein in his temper before he went after her and delivered the set-down she deserved.

As Rowan banged through the cupboards for a kettle she trembled with outrage.

And fear. If her mother and Olief were really gone…

Her breath stalled at how adrift that left her. She'd come here to find some point to her life, some direction. She'd made quite a mess of things in the last year, she'd give Nic that, but she needed time to sort it all out and make a plan for her future. Big, sure, heartless Nic didn't seem to want to give her that, though.

He pushed into the room, his formidable presence like a shove into deeper water. She gripped the edge of the bench, resenting him with every bone in her body. She wouldn't let him do this to her.

"I don't know why I'm surprised," she seethed. "You don't have a sensitive bone in your body. You're made up of icicles, aren't you?"

He jerked his head back. "Better that than the slots of a piggy bank," he returned with frost. "It's not Olief being gone that worries you, but his deep pockets—isn't it?"

"I'm not the one taking over his offices and bank accounts, am I? What's wrong? The board giving you a hard time again? Maybe you shouldn't have been so quick to jump into Olief's shoes like you owned them."

"Who else could be trusted?" he shot back. "The board wanted to sell off pieces for their personal gain. I kept it intact so Olief would have something to come back to."

She'd been aware in those early weeks of him warring with Olief's top investors, but she'd had her own struggles with rehabilitating her leg. The corporation had been the last thing on her mind.

"I've looked for them even while sitting at his desk," Nic continued. "I paid searchers long after the authorities gave up. What did *you* do?" he challenged. "Keep your mother's fan club rabid and frenzied?"

Rowan curled her toes in the tight leather of her boots, stabbed with inadequacy and affront. "My leg was broken. I couldn't get out in a boat to look for them. And doing all those interviews wasn't a cakewalk!"

He snorted. "Blinking back manufactured tears was difficult, was it?"

Manufactured? She always fought back tears when she couldn't avoid facing the reality of that lost plane. Snapping her head to the side, she refused to let him see how talking about the disappearance upset her. He obviously didn't see her reaction as sincere and she wasn't about to beg him to believe her.

Especially when she had very mixed feelings—some

that scared her. Guilt turned in her like a spool of barbed wire as she thought of the many times she had wished she could be out from under her mother's controlling thumb. Since turning nineteen she had been waffling constantly between outright defiance that would have cut all ties to Cassandra O'Brien and a desire to stay close to Olief, Rosedale—and, she admitted silently, with a suffocating squeeze of mortification, within the sphere of Olief's black sheep son.

But she hadn't wished Cassandra O'Brien would *die*.

She couldn't declare her mother dead. It was sick. Wrong. Rowan swiped her clammy palms over the seat of her jeans before running water into the kettle. She wouldn't do it.

"If you want to run Olief's enterprise, fill your boots," she said shakily. "But if all you want is more control over it, and by extension *me*, don't expect me to help you." She set the kettle to boil, then risked a glance at him.

He wore the most painfully supercilious smirk. "I'm willing to forgive your debts to gain your cooperation," he levied.

"My debts?" she repeated laughingly. "A few months of credit card bills?" She and her mother had been in worse shape dozens of times. *"We're in dire straits, love. Be a good girl and dance us out."* Appearance fees were a sordid last resort, but Rowan wasn't above it. "You'll have to do better than that," she said coldly.

He leaned a well-muscled arm on the refrigerator. His laconic stance and wide chest, so unashamedly male, made her mouth go dry.

"Name your price, then."

His confidence was as compelling as his physique, and all the more aggravating because she didn't possess any immunity to it. She wanted to put a crack in his composure.

"Rosedale," she tossed out. It was a defiant challenge, but earnest want crept into her tone. This was her home. This was where Olief would return...if he could.

"Rosedale?" Nic repeated.

His frigid stare gave her a shiver of apprehension before she reminded herself she was being crass because he was.

She tensed her sooty lashes into protective slits as she held his intimidating gaze. "Why not?" she challenged. "You don't want it."

"Not true. I don't like the *house*," he corrected, shifting his big body into an uncompromising stance, shoulders pinned back, arms folded in refusal. "The location is perfect, though. I intend to tear down this monstrosity as soon as it's emptied and build something that suits me better. So, no, you may not have Rosedale."

"Tear it down?" The words hissed in her throat like the steam off the kettle. "Why would you even threaten such a thing? Just to hurt me?"

"Hurt you?" He frowned briefly. Any hint of softening was dismissed in a blink. "Don't try to manipulate me with your acts of melodrama, Rowan. No, I'm not doing anything *to* you. You're not on my radar enough for me to be that personal."

Of course not. And she shouldn't let him so far into her psyche that she was scorched by that. But there he was, making her burn with humiliation and hurt.

"Unlike you, I don't play games," he continued. "That wasn't a threat. It's the truth. The house is completely impractical. If I'm going to live here I want open rooms, more access to the outdoors, fewer stairs."

"Then don't live here!"

"Athens has been my base most of my life. It's a short helicopter or boat trip from here to there. The island's vineyard is profitable in its own right, which I'm sure is the real reason you want your hands on the place, but I'm not going to hand you a property worth multi-millions because your mother slept her way into having a ridiculous house built on it. What I *will* do is allow you to take whatever Cassandra left here—if you do it in a timely manner."

Rowan could only stare into his emotionless blue eyes. His gall left her speechless. Her mind could barely comprehend all he was saying. Rosedale gone? Pick over her mother's things like she was snatching bargains at a yard sale? Give up *hope*?

A stabbing pain drove through her, spreading an ache like poison across her chest and lifting a sting into her throat and behind her eyes.

"I don't want *things*, Nic. I want my home and my family!"

She was going to cry, and it was the last thing she could bear to do in front of this glacier-veined man. It was more like her to go toe-to-toe than run from a fight, but for the second time in half an hour she had to walk out on him.

After hiking the length of the island in heels, her feet refused a visit to all her favored haunts, so Rowan went as far as the sandy shoreline and kicked off her boots. The water was higher than she'd ever seen it, but she usually only swam in summer, rarely came to the beach in winter, and she hadn't been looking at the water when she'd followed Nic down here two years ago.

Wincing, she turned her mind from that debacle—only to become conscious of how grim a place the beach was to visit since her mother and Olief had likely drowned somewhere out there in the Mediterranean. One year ago.

She was starting to hate this time of year.

Starting up the beach, she tried to escape the hitch of guilt catching in her, not wanting to dwell on how she'd

asked them to come for her when she'd broken her leg. She
hadn't been able to go to them—not physically and, more
significantly, because she had feared running into Nic.

Oh, that hateful man! She hated him all the more for
having a point. He wasn't *right*, but she had to acknowledge he wasn't completely wrong. She hadn't expected to
find her mother and Olief in residence, but she'd wanted
to feel close to them as she faced the anniversary of their
disappearance and accepted what he'd come out and said:
it was very unlikely they would ever come back and tell
her what to do.

The rest of her life stretched before her like the water,
endless and formless. Until the dance school had kicked
her out she'd never faced anything like this. Logically she
knew she ought to celebrate this freedom and opportunity,
but it looked so empty.

Her life was empty. She had no one.

Rowan drank salt-scented air as she inhaled, trying to
ease the constriction in her lungs. Not yet. She didn't have
to face all that until the year was officially up. Nic could
go to hell with his court documents and demands that she
face reality.

As she contemplated dealing with his threats against
Rosedale a moment of self-pity threatened. Why did he
dislike her so much? His cloud of harsh judgment always
seemed directed inexorably toward her, but why? They
were nothing to each other. He might be Olief's son, but
who would know it? He only ever referred to Olief by
name, never even in conversation as "my father," yet he
wanted the rights of a son, full inheritance. That egotisti-
cal sense of privilege affronted her. She wanted to stand
up for Olief if for no other reason than that Nic didn't deserve the position of sole heir. He'd never made a proper

effort to be part of the family, and he wasn't looking out for what was left of it: *her*.

Estranged seemed to be his preferred option in any relationship. That wall of detachment had broken Olief's heart. And it made Rowan nervous because it made Nic formidable. Her insides clenched at the thought of Rosedale being torn down. She couldn't lose her home.

Reaching the end of the beach, where a long flat rock created the edge of the cove, she clambered up to a well-used vantage point. The waves were wild, coming in with a wind that tore at her hair and peppered her with sea spray. Barnacles cut into her bare soles while bits of kelp in icy tide pools made for slippery steps in between.

She picked her way to the edge, reveling in the struggle to reach it under the ferocious mood of the sky. Another wave smashed against the rocks under her toes, high enough to spray her thighs and wash bitter swirls of cold water around her ankles before it was sucked back to open water. Uncomfortable, but not enough to chase her away.

Throwing back her head, she sent out a challenge to the gathering storm as if standing up to Nic. "I won't let you scare me off!"

The words were tossed away on a whistling wind, but it felt good to say them. To stand firm against the crash and gush and pull of a wintry sea that soaked her calves before dragging at the denim in retreat.

It wasn't until a third monster, higher than all the rest, rolled in and exploded in a wall of water, soaking her to the chest, that she realized she might not be strong enough to win against such a mighty enemy.

If Rowan thought he'd bring her luggage out of the rain or pour her tea while she stamped around outside throwing a hissy fit, she had another think coming. Nic went upstairs to his office and did his best to dismiss her from his mind.

It didn't go well. That heartbreaking catch in her voice when she'd said, "*I want my home and my family*," kept ringing in his mind, making him uncomfortable.

He wasn't close to his own mother, and after many times hearing Rowan and Cassandra fight like cats in a cage had assumed their relationship was little better than an armed truce. Of course he'd observed over the years that regard for one's parents was fairly universal, and he obviously would have preferred it if Olief had survived rather than disappeared, but he hadn't imagined Rowan was feeling deep distress over any of this. Her anguish startled him. Throughout this entire year, as always, he had tried not to think much of her at all—certainly not to dwell on how she was coping emotionally.

He coped by working long hours and avoiding deep thoughts altogether. Getting emotional and wishing for the impossible was a waste of time. Nothing could be changed by angst and hand-wringing.

Moving to the window, he tried to escape doing anything of that sort now, telling himself he was only observing the weather. On the horizon, the haze of an angry front was drawing in. It was the storm that had been promised when he'd checked the weather report, and the reason he'd come over last night on the yacht rather than trying to navigate choppy, possibly deadly seas today.

A storm like this had taken down Olief's plane. He and Cassandra had been off to fetch Rowan from yet another of her madcap adventures. *She* was the reason Nic had no chance of knowing Olief or grasping the seemingly simple concept she'd bandied about at him so easily: *family*. Rowan might not be the whole reason, but one way or another she had interfered with Nic's efforts to get to know his father. She had demanded Olief's attention with cheeky misbehavior and constant bids for attention, interrupting whenever Nic found a moment with the man and constantly distracting him with her unrelenting sex appeal. He'd had to walk away from progress a thousand times. Away from her.

Prickling with antipathy, he unconsciously scanned the places he'd most often observed her over the years, not aware he was looking for her until he felt a twinge of confusion when he didn't find her where he usually would. She wasn't at the gazebo or up the hilltop or on the beach—

He spotted her and swore. *Fool.*

Bare feet had been a bad idea. Rowan couldn't move fast across the sharp, uneven rocks to outrun the tide that was coming in with inescapable resolve. She couldn't even see where she was stepping. The water had come in deep enough to eddy around her knees, keeping her off balance. With her arms flapping, she silently begged her mum and Olief, *If you can hear me, please help me get back to shore alive.*

The response to her plea was the biggest wave yet, visible as a steel-gray wall crawling up behind her with ominous size and strength. Rowan dug in with her numb toes and braced for impact. Her whole body shuddered as the weight of the water began to climb her already soaked clothes, gathering height as it loomed behind her.

She held her breath.

The wave broke at her shoulders and with a cry she felt herself thrown forward onto what felt like broken glass. Her hands and knees felt the scrape of barnacles as she tried to scramble for purchase, but then she was lifted. Her heart stopped. The wave was going to roll her across these rocks before it dragged her out to die.

Rowan clawed toward the surface long enough to get a glimpse of Nic running flat out down the beach.

"Ni—" Her mouth filled with water.

Nic lost sight of her as the surf thundered into itself. He pushed his body to the limit, tormented anger bubbling like acid inside him. Questions pounded with his footsteps digging across the wet sand. What did God have against him? Why did he have to lose everything? Why *her*—?

An arm flailed, fighting to stay in the foam that drained off the ledge of rocks. If the retreating wave carried her into deeper water she'd be thrown back into the rocks with the next surge that came in. Rowan fought for her life and so did Nic. He leapt onto the ledge and waded into the turbulence, able to read the terror on her face as she valiantly fought to keep herself from being pulled beyond reach.

At the last second she surged forward enough that he was able to clamp his hand on her wrist. He dragged her up and out of the water, clutching her to his chest as he made for safer ground. The tide poured in with another wave big enough to soak his seat and spatter his back before he reached the sand and finally the grass. He stopped, heart racing with exertion, too close to seeing her die to ease his vice-like grip.

Rowan clung tightly to Nic even as he crushed her, stunned by how close she'd come to being sucked into certain death. She was shocked to the core that he'd arrived at just the right time to help her. Astounded that he'd bothered.

He hadn't hesitated, though. His clothes were as soaked as her own, his heart pounding as loud and rapidly as hers. As her senses crept back to a functioning state she realized how thoroughly she was plastered to him. They were embracing like soulmates.

She lifted her face from the hollow of his shoulder, but his arms remained iron-hard, pinning her to a chest roped with muscle, holding her so close she could smell faded aftershave and sea spray. Warmth crept into the seam of their bodies, spilling a teasing pleasure under her skin wherever their wet clothes adhered.

Gratitude. She tried dismissing it. But it was more. It didn't matter that she'd been here two years ago, very close to this place on the beach, and had received a harsh set down on the heels of experiencing this same rush. Nic was the only man to affect her like this, no matter how often she'd dated or tried to let other men arouse her. Nic had set the bar impossibly high when she'd first begun noticing the opposite sex. She had yet to find anyone who measured up. It meant that his arms were the ones she secretly longed to feel around her. Now he was ruining her even more, because the fit of her body to his was so perfect. The flood of tingling awareness so exciting.

His gaze caught her own and stillness came over him. She mentally braced herself, but instead of fury something hot flickered in his eyes. His expression darkened with a flush that almost looked like— Rowan caught her breath, confused. *Lust?* Impossible. He hated her.

Nevertheless, she could feel an unmistakable male reaction against her abdomen. An answering trickle of desire made her wriggle her hips in embarrassed curiosity.

His arms hardened, holding her still for his penetrating gaze as their mutual reaction became undeniable. He knew she was getting turned on. He was turned on and was forcing her to acknowledge it.

Her mind blanked as her unsteady heart kicked into overdrive. She'd been drunk the last time, and insulated against what had really been happening. The moon behind him had kept his face in shadow. He'd kissed her, angrily, and then had pushed her away as fast as he'd yanked her close.

This hadn't happened. Rowan was a skilled flirt, ever conscious of the power of her sex appeal, but real sexual need had never ignited in her properly. She'd never felt another man's arousal and been intrigued and excited. She'd always kept a clear head and been able to put on the brakes.

Not now. She longed to let Nic support her as she melted in abject surrender.

Panicked by her dwindling willpower, she pushed against his chest. "What are you doing?" she sputtered. The power of his spell glinted like fairy dust around her, disorienting her. Perhaps she'd fantasized from afar too long. She was seeing things that weren't there. Nic had never shown any kind of desire for her. Where had his arousal come from? Why now?

Nic's half-step back was by his choice, not her forceful shove, and now his grim expression held none of the heat she had thought she'd seen. If anything, he seemed vaguely disgusted. A cloak of reserve fell around him, turning him into the distant, condescending man she'd always known.

"I'm saving your life. What were you thinking, climbing out there when the water is this high?"

"Everyone climbs out there," she excused, wondering if she'd imagined that brief press of hard male flesh. Wishful thinking? Hardly. Getting into bed with this man would be like climbing into a cage with a tiger. When she finally slept with someone she'd choose a domesticated housecat. "How was I supposed to know the waves would come up like that? It's never happened before." She crossed her arms, feeling her soaked clothes and wet hair as the wind cut through her. Her chin rattled and she shivered.

"It's called a tide table and a weather report, Rowan." He kept his gaze locked onto the horizon, his jaw like iron.

"Anyone reading tide tables in their leisure time is in danger of drowning in boredom. Who *does* that?"

"I checked both before bringing the yacht over yesterday," he said stiffly, barely glancing at her as he added derisively, "Anyone who ignores basic precautions deserves the natural selection that results."

"Then why didn't you let nature take its course with me today?" she groused. The bottom of the Med sounded infinitely more comfortable than suffering a lecture while turning into an ice pop.

A barely discernible flinch was gone before she was sure she'd really seen it.

His face hardened into an inscrutable mask as he glared out to sea. "You disappearing along with the others would look suspicious. I have to keep you alive long enough to sign the documents I brought. Since I just did you a very solid favor, you'll comply." His blue eyes came back to her with freezing resolve.

"Dream on," she retorted, but he was already turning away, everything in him dismissive of her and sure of his success.

Annoyed beyond measure, she stayed where she was, longing to be stubborn. But it was cold out here. Other sensations were penetrating as well. Her hands and feet burned along with her knee. The denim was torn out of her jeans on her bad leg, exposing bloody, scraped skin. Her palms were rashed raw and cuts on her fingers welled with blood. The bottoms of her feet felt as if they'd been branded.

Sickened, she lifted her head to call Nic, but he was without sympathy, striding away without a backward glance, his wet clothes clinging to his form as he rounded the hedge and disappeared. He didn't care if she was hurt. He had his own agenda.

Grimly aware she had no one else to call for help, she gritted her teeth and limped her way back to the house.

CHAPTER THREE

"Why didn't you let nature take its course with me?" Nic was still sizzling when he left the shower, deeply angered by Rowan's remark. She was internally programmed to make flippant, provocative comments, so he shouldn't give her the satisfaction of getting a rise out of him, but today she was under his skin more than ever—and he'd been fighting his attraction toward her since before it had even been sexual.

He paused in hitching a towel around his wet hips, thinking back to those early years when she'd been a nubile sprite, too young for any man let alone one sowing the wild oats of his early twenties. Even so, she'd flitted in and out of his awareness with irritating persistence. He'd been alternately fascinated and annoyed, drawn by her quick wit even while baffled at the way she took it for granted that everyone loved her—especially Olief.

He'd been perversely determined not to fall under her spell, too irritated by how easily everything came to her. At a similar age, Nic had spent his holidays haunting the empty rooms of his boarding school. Olief hadn't wanted his wife to know about his indiscretion, so Nic hadn't entered the man's world until the woman had died and Cassandra had come on the scene. *Her* indiscretion had had an open invitation to spend school breaks in Olief's house. As an afterthought Nic had been asked to join them, but he'd been traveling by then, shedding light on the world's darkest injustices, inexplicably drawn into following Olief's footsteps into hard-hitting news journalism.

When Nic had come to Rosedale after those stints abroad it hadn't been for happy family time. In one way, at least, Olief had understood Nic. Olief had recognized Nic's need to retreat somewhere remote and quiet because Olief had experienced a similar need himself when he'd done that sort of work. The island's tranquility had kept Nic coming here, but the visits hadn't been comfortable—not when Olief showered affection on Rowan and she dominated everyone's attention.

Nic had done everything in his power to ignore and resist her, but she'd still managed to penetrate his shield. He was standing here because of her, wasn't he? Veering from deep insult that she'd actually thought he would leave her to die to stark fear at how close a call she'd had. That near miss unsettled him more than he wanted to admit. He told himself it was its similarity to the other deaths that made his blood run cold, but on the heels of that thought came the recollection that his blood hadn't stayed cold. He'd nearly let nature take its course in the form of raw, debaucherous lust.

His groin tightened in remembrance of the feel of her, the press of her hips.

Idiot. Revealing his weakness had been a mistake. He hadn't meant to, but the cork had popped under the pressure of saving her from danger and finally, after two years of reimagining it, holding her.

Bloody hell—why did she have to feel tailor-made for his form? The perfect height. A slender yet curvaceous shape that could wrap around him without smothering his need for space and autonomy. Her breasts, as natural as

God had made them, had crushed against his chest with nipples so hardened by the cold he'd felt them like pebbles through both their shirts. He clenched his fists, still longing to warm those tight peaks with his tongue until they were both hot all through.

Naked, and burningly aroused, he tilted back his head and struggled against the foe that had been stalking him for too long. He didn't recall when the switch had happened. Sometime between hearing she'd been caught with a boy at school and seeing her climb from the pool at eighteen. Suddenly he'd been unable to ignore her, or the singe in his blood whenever he was around her.

Then she had turned twenty, drunk her way to the bottom of a champagne bottle and, with no other man in the vicinity, turned her wiles on him.

Nic had tried not to let temptation get the better of him. He'd at least gone to the beach to avoid her. She'd followed, determined to get her man.

Nic had rules. Drunk women were never on the menu, no matter how willing they appeared to be. She'd sidled up to him, though, and he'd succumbed to a moment of weakness. One kiss. One warning to a reckless young woman who needed a lesson in putting herself at a man's mercy. One peek through the door into carnal paradise.

And Olief had seen it from the house. He hadn't seen Nic push her away, hadn't heard Nic read her the Riot Act. By the time Olief had reached the beach Rowan had been stumbling her way back to the house, and Nic had finally earned a hard-won moment of privacy with Olief.

It had been punctured by words Nic would never forget. *"What are your intentions, Nic? Marriage?"*

Olief's appalled disbelief, sharp with disparagement, had cut through Nic. It had been more than Olief warning off an experienced man from what he considered an impressionable young woman, deluded as that judgment had been. There'd been a fleck of challenge—as if Olief couldn't believe Nic would dare contemplate marrying into his family; as if he looked down on Nic for imagining it would be allowed. Nic wasn't good enough to be acknowledged as his son. Did he really imagine Olief would accept him as a son-in-law? Where did he get the nerve even to consider it?

It had been worse than humiliating. It had been hurtful. To this day Nic suspected Rowan had set up the whole thing and he wanted to shake her for it.

And yet when he'd had his hands on her today he'd only wanted to feel more of her. He'd seen the glow of arousal seep under Rowan's skin and that had been a fresh, sharp aphrodisiac. The volcano of lust pulsing in him refused to abate now he'd caught a glimpse of answering fire in her, hotter and more acutely aware than he'd ever seen it in her before. Damn it, she was—

What?

He opened his eyes but saw nothing, still blinded by hunger even as a shift occurred in his psyche. She wasn't too young. Not anymore.

Off-limits? By whose standards? Olief's? He was dead, and if he were alive to know how many men Rowan had had, he wouldn't defend her as being inexperienced.

As to marriage—well, Nic didn't want to marry anyone. Especially Rowan. He wanted to slake this hunger and move on with his life.

Nic winced, hearing his rationalizations for what they were, but craving was clawing in his chest, tearing through the walls of resistance he'd kept in place through years of encounters with her. Possibility opened before him with treacherous appeal. What was to stop him? Nothing. There was nothing to keep him from having her. Why shouldn't he? She'd been throwing herself at him for years.

Nic shuddered with physical need and inner turmoil. He never acted on impulse, yet everything in him longed to hunt her down right now and *take*. He shook off wild yearning and reached for self-discipline. Cool logic. Self-respect. He loathed her. Coming to Rosedale wasn't about giving in to an appetite he'd denied for years. It was about gaining what he really wanted: his rightful place as the head of Olief's media conglomerate. Not because he was the man's son, but because he'd earned it.

Nic shrugged into a light pullover and faded jeans, trying to ignore his unrelenting want for Rowan, searching for a clear mind while opportunity hung before him, refusing to be disregarded.

What a profound thorn in his vitals she was. She would never sign those papers if she thought she could string him along by torturing his libido.

His body aching with denial, he gathered his wet clothes and faced the inconvenience of Anna's quitting. Doing the washing and other chores would be a good lesson for Rowan, he decided arrogantly. Perhaps he was looking to punish her after all. She had been tormenting him for years. He was entitled to payback. At the very least she'd learn this wasn't rent-free accommodation.

He was framing exactly how he'd inform her of that when the bloody footprints in the upper hall stopped him cold.

Rowan jerked her head out of the shower spray. *Nic?*

"What the hell? Rowan!" His voice grew louder. The bathroom door opened and he was right there on the other side of the steamed glass, glaring like an angry drill sergeant.

Rowan squeaked in shock and turned her back on him, but she couldn't ignore the fact she was stark naked in front of him. The underside of her skin began to warm even though she was still frozen at her core. She tensed her buttocks, aware her bottom was on blatant display. Since when did he even know which room she used?

Strategically hugging herself, she cried, "Get out of here!"

"What have you done? It looks like a crime scene out there!"

"Oh, did I stain the precious hardwood you're planning to tear up? I'll scrub it once I quit bleeding to death, I promise. Now, get out!"

The door slammed with firm disgust. She sniffed in disdain at his impossible standards and stared at hands that looked worse under the running water. They scorched with protest at the pummel of spray, but they had to be cleaned. Her feet were begging her to get off them, but her leg worried her most. Not the sting on her skin, which was acute enough to make her clench her back molars. No, there was a deeper pain that concerned her. All the walking today hadn't helped. She was afraid to look but had to. No one else would.

Rolling her eyes at her decline into maudlin self-pity, she switched off the shower and dragged a bathsheet around herself. It wasn't as if her mother would be any use in this situation so why bother getting weepy? Olief would have been solicitous, though.

Shaking off wistfulness, still deeply chilled, she closed the lid of the toilet and sat down to pat herself dry. The door swung open again.

"Really?" she demanded, instinctively curling her feet in and closing a hand over the knot of her towel. She was in a high enough state of turmoil without Nic accosting her with his potent male energy every ten seconds. He'd already got her all bewildered on the beach, and then seen her naked in the shower. Sitting on a toilet in a bathsheet, shaking off a near-death experience, put her at the worst disadvantage ever.

He hesitated at the door, but it wasn't with doubt. She had the impression he was gathering himself. Bracing for a challenge.

Odd. She searched his expression for more clues, but he revealed nothing beyond a clinical interest in her hands as he set bandages and disinfectant on the counter. "You scraped yourself on the rocks, I assume?"

"Good work, Holmes. I should have consulted government-issued safe work plans prior to retreating from the tide, I assume?"

A pithy look, then, "It's a wonder your mother didn't drown you at birth. Do you want help or not?"

She grudgingly held out a hand. "I don't even know why you want to help me."

"I don't," he replied flatly, going down on one knee and reaching for supplies. "But I am an adult, and adults take responsibility rather than doing whatever selfish thing they want."

"Is that a dig? Because I'm almost twenty-two. A fully-fledged adult." Even to herself she sounded like a petulant child and, really, reminding him it was nearly her birthday was the last thing she ought to do.

"All grown up," he said, with an ironic twist to the corner of his mouth. Renewed tension seemed to gather in his expression as he smoothed a bandage against her wrist.

"Yes," she claimed pertly. Her pulse involuntarily tripped under his dispassionate caress, making her subtly catch a breath.

His gaze came up sharply, the blue like the center of a flame.

She was transported back to the feel of his arms as they'd stood wet and trembling on the beach, his arousal hardening against her. Heat flooded into her, chasing away the last of her chill, cooking her alive. She should have felt appalled and disgusted, but to her eternal shame she was energized by the crackle of sexual awareness in the air.

"All grown up," he repeated, with flint in his tone, and lifted her hand to press his lips against the bandage, a cruelly mocking glint in his eye.

She flinched and pulled her hand away, even though she'd barely felt the pressure of his mouth. That *so* hadn't been kiss-and-make-it-better!

Derisive amusement darkened his eyes. "No? That's not like you, Ro."

Her heart took a long plunge of disgrace. At the same time she felt herself begin to glow with heated longing and other weakening sensations, even as uncertainty and intrigue muddled her mind. Desperately she reminded herself of how unaffected and ruthless he could be.

"What are you doing, Nic?" she asked, trying unsuccessfully to clear the huskiness from her throat. "Offering a clumsy seduction in hopes of getting what you want out of me?"

"Oh, I'm far from clumsy. I know exactly what I'm doing when it comes to seduction." The hard tone was coupled with a look that might as well have swept the towel from her body and left her as nude as she'd been in the shower.

Had she really wished over the years for him to notice her? *Really* notice her? This was a horribly defenseless feeling! Every single occasion of testing a flirty glance or enticing him with a smile came back to her as mortifyingly obvious behavior that was now giving him the chance to get the better of her.

"You're having a go at me," she accused, as much to remind herself as to let him know she saw through him. "I'm sure other women wither at your feet when you bring your best game, but I'm not one of them. Act solicitous all you want, but I know you don't care. You don't want me. You don't even like me."

He took a moment to smooth a plaster over her second palm, finally asking with detached interest, "Do all of those things have to be in place at once?" He met her gaze with a look of cool consideration.

She pressed her lips into a tight line, stung by the implied agreement that he didn't like her. Yet still wanted her. That shouldn't excite her, but her blood seemed to slow and thicken in her arteries, making her feel hot and full of power.

"Since when did you even think about me before you decided I was in the way of something you wanted?" she managed, trying to ignore the internal signals bouncing with anticipation inside her.

His shoulders went back and his jaw hardened. "One has nothing to do with the other. I may want you to sign some papers, but that has nothing to do with physical chemistry."

"Chemistry that cropped up today of all days?" she scoffed, flushing with anger because her reaction to him had been torturing her forever. "It certainly wasn't there two years ago, was it?" she prodded, thinking, *Shut up, Rowan*.

"You want to go back to that?" With a flash of the tested anger he'd shown her then, he reached forward to cup the back of her wet head and pulled her forward to meet the crush of his mouth over hers.

"N-n-n...!" She almost got the word out, but it turned

into a whimper of surprise, then disintegrated under the assertive rake of his very knowledgeable mouth.

No champagne or the romance of a windswept beach this time. This was raw, unapologetic and incredibly beguiling. He kissed with the same command and purpose that emanated from the rest of his being. *He* was in control. *He* would take what he wanted. Their last kiss and the biting lecture that had followed had been a warning she should have heeded. Nic was a powerful, dangerous man.

Who knew how to level a woman with a kiss.

She brought her hands to his wrist and shoulder, overwhelmed yet helpless to the enthralling press of his lips over hers. There was no fighting him as he took her mouth—not because he was stronger, but because he made it so good. She could practically taste his contempt, his selfish demand that she give up everything to him, but there was skill here, too. A wicked appeal to the primitive in her. He drew her into the kiss even when she knew she shouldn't let herself be drawn.

Her inner being expanded toward him, tendrils of heated pleasure reaching for connection. She moaned, unfamiliar imperatives climbing with primal force in her. This was Nic. He didn't want her. He was messing with her. But this was *Nic*. She'd fantasized about him for years.

The light scrape of his teeth suffused her with heat. The proprietorial thrust of his tongue, the captivating taste of his mouth over hers, stabbed excitement through her, nudging her into a dark world of wild sensations and ravenous desire. Her limbs curled toward him like stems toward the sun, wanting more. It was crazy. Distantly she recognized this possession of her mouth had a purpose: arousal. He intended to take her all the way.

Her heart skipped. She shouldn't let this happen, but she wanted to. And he wasn't a force to be stopped. He reached to her lower back and pulled her hips toward him, forcing her knees to part and bracket his waist. Her shin struck the register. A ringing pain slashed through her wanton stupor, making her jolt in shock. Her towel slipped.

Oh, God, what was she *doing*?

Nic checked the urge to overpower Rowan's recoil and drag her back into the kiss. Into the bedroom or onto the floor. Anywhere. She was flushed, and her breath was stuttering from between glossy kiss-swollen lips. Her eyes were still cloudy with desire, the honeyed taste of her sexual appetite still tangible on his tongue.

The beast ran hard in him, fighting against being steered back into its corral. Nic's chest heaved and the hot coil of pressure behind his fly demanded release. He had one hand braced on the wall and used the other to reach for her jaw, ignoring the mental warnings trying to penetrate his fog of carnal hunger. This time he'd let it happen.

Before he could tilt Rowan back into the direction they'd been headed, her pale expression and the flash of a worried look downward stopped him. She leaned cautiously to examine her leg, her hand pressing the middle of his chest to push him back.

He followed her gaze and the sight froze him. Not the scrape on her knee. That was little worse than a tumble off a bicycle would produce, but the scars down her shin were horrific.

"What the hell?" He sat back on his heels, physical arousal taking a backseat to shock. The depth of her injury, communicated by the crisscross of thin white lines, revolted him. He reached one hand behind her knee and had to school his clenching muscles to take care as he lifted her ankle in the other hand, studying the full extent of the damage.

Her shin wasn't the only issue. She had old scars all over her feet, framing knobbly toes with cracked nails that were only partially healed.

Rowan flexed her foot. "Don't."

"Hurts?" It had to. The marks spoke of repeated injuries.

She snorted. "I've lived with pain at that end of my body for so long I don't even notice it. I don't like anyone looking at my feet." Her lashes swept down in self-conscious dismay. "They're ugly."

"They're not pretty," he agreed, smoothing the pad of his thumb over an old callus, astounded by the time and effort it would have required to form the thick bump. "This is from dancing?"

"We all get them," she defended, and attempted to pull from his grip.

He held on. He hadn't meant to sound so appalled, but he was inexplicably angered. The big scar was bad enough, but at least it was understandable. It had been an accident. These others…

"Why would anyone do this to herself?" he questioned, channeling an unexpected surge of concern into impatience. "I've seen foot soldiers coming off a month-long march with better feet."

She flushed and pushed her damp hair behind her ear. "It's part of the process. They've gotten a lot better since I've been off them."

"Because your leg was broken." He looked again at the long scar. Everything Rowan did was superficial, but suddenly he couldn't be dismissive of what she'd been going through. Her remark about being in constant pain echoed in his head along with her old claims of *"doing the best I can"* to Cassandra's livid, *"How can you not be ready?"*

It occurred to him that his impression of Rowan as a slacker was largely based on those overheard accusations that Rowan wasn't trying hard enough. That perturbed him. He generally formed his own opinions, but he'd been seeing her with a skewed view to hold her at a distance. He didn't often mislead himself like that.

"How many surgeries have you had?" he asked, setting her cut foot on his thigh.

"Three. I'm a little concerned about the pins, actually," she confided hesitantly. "I think they're killing me right now because they got cold. Does anything feel out of place?" She bit her lip, the apprehensive pull of her brow more concerning than her actual words. She was suppressing very real distress.

A chill took him as he carefully felt up and down her calf. The male in him was aware of lean muscle under smooth pale skin, and fascinating shadows beneath the drape of the bathsheet across her thighs. He'd got a too brief glimpse of her through the steamed walls of the shower and was dying for a proper study of her form. He focused on determining whether she'd rebroken something, but that thought filled the pit of his stomach with ashes—not unlike the defeated fury that had taken him as he'd run up the beach, afraid he wouldn't reach her in time.

He turned his mind from that raw terror.

"It seems okay. Will you dance again?" He already knew the answer, and tension gathered in him, resisting the truth.

She leaned forward to palpate the shin herself, brushing his hands off her calf, remaining silent. He lifted his gaze from watching her massage her torn muscles. Her mink lashes formed a pair of tangled lines.

"On tables," she finally replied with a tough smile, "but not on the stage."

Expecting the answer didn't make it easier to hear. He was taken aback by a surprisingly sharp stab of sympathy. As a journalist, he'd spent his life asking people for their reactions to events, but he had never asked anyone *How do you feel about that*? He wanted to ask Rowan, but her snarky response grated, compelling him to say, "You never wanted to dance anyway. It was a bone of contention with your mother, wasn't it? Her insisting you go to that fancy school? You must be relieved."

She gave a little snort of cynical amusement and dipped her head in a single nod that left her damp hair hanging. "Yes, I can honestly say I was relieved when they finally admitted I would never get back to my old level and asked me to leave so someone with whole bones and genuine passion could take my spot."

His heart kicked as he disagreed with *anyone* claiming Rowan lacked passion. He was still tingling from their kiss a minute ago. He didn't let the sensation escalate, though, sidetracked by her bitter revelation.

"When *they* admitted?" he repeated. "You wanted to quit and they wanted to rehabilitate you?" He reached for a bandage to cover her knee, aware of his sympathy dwindling. She *was* a shirker after all.

"Madame is a close friend of Mum's. She knew Mum wouldn't want all those years of training to be for nothing, but she also knew as well as I did that I had reached my potential before the accident and that I'd never be good enough. She pushed me anyway, and I tried until my ankle gave out. We finally agreed I was a grand failure and the silver lining was that my mother would never know."

He didn't want to be affected by the wounded shadows of defeat lurking behind her sparking eyes and pugnacious chin, but he was. Rowan might have quit, but because she was a realist about her own limitations, not a quitter. He wondered what else he'd failed to see in her before today.

"If you didn't like dance, why did you pursue it?" he asked.

A brief pause, then a challenging, "Why did *you* go into the same field as Olief?"

It was a blatant deflection from his own question—one that deepened his interest in her motives. He answered her first, though. His reason was simple enough.

"I was curious about him so I followed his work. You can't read that many articles on world events and not feel compelled to discover the next chapter." He shrugged and began patching her other knee. "I wasn't trying to emulate him. Were you? Trying to emulate Cassandra?"

Rowan made a noise of scorn. "Not by choice. Count yourself lucky that no one knew you were related to Olief when you started out. You were able to prove yourself on your own merit and do it because you wanted to. I was pushed into dancing as a gag. It was a way for my mother to stand out, because she had this little reflection of herself beside her. She was allowed to quit when she and Olief got together, but I still had all this 'potential' to be realized."

Nic had never framed his abandonment by his parents as good fortune, but he'd never taken a hard look at Rowan's situation and seen it for misfortune either.

He frowned, not enjoying the sense that he'd been blind and wrong. None of Rowan's revelations changed anything, he reminded himself. He still wanted full control of Marcussen Media. She still needed to sign the petition forms, grow up, and take responsibility for herself—not party her way across Europe at his expense.

Rowan watched Nic's concentration on her fade to something more familiar and removed and suspected she knew why. She dropped her gaze to the bandaged hands she'd clenched in her lap, the fetid crown of disloyalty making her hang her head. In her wildest dreams she had never imagined Nic would be the person to crack this resentment out of her. She'd anticipated taking her anger to the grave, because only the lowest forms of life said anything against Cassandra O'Brien. A good daughter would certainly never betray her mother when she was *gone*.

"Not that I hated her for forcing me into it," Rowan mumbled, trying to recant. "I understood. She was my age when she had me. All she knew was performing, and that sort of career doesn't wait around while you raise a child. She didn't have any support. Her family disowned her when she left to become—*gasp!*—an actress. You have to be an opportunist to survive in that business, and that's what she was trying to do. Survive."

She risked a glance upward and saw that Nic didn't exactly look sympathetic. He was closing off completely to what she was saying, his lip curling in cynical understanding of words like "opportunist" and "survivor."

Rowan clenched her teeth, thinking she would be calling on all the skills Cassandra O'Brien had ever taught her when it came to surviving. That had been the real source of animosity between mother and daughter: the things Cassandra had done to keep them both fed and clothed. The men she'd brought into their home—the homes she'd brought Rowan into. The pressure for Rowan to 'make it' so they had a fallback position if things went south. The fact that when it came right down to it Cassandra had been most concerned about her own survival at the expense of her daughter's happiness, and had alternately been threatened by and quick to exploit her daughter's youth and beauty.

The tenderness of pressure on a cut pulled Rowan back to Nic pressing a bandage into place on the bottom of her foot.

"What are you going to do now?" he asked.

"That's the million-dollar question, isn't it? I'm not exactly brimming with marketable skills."

"Perhaps you should have addressed that as soon as you left school, rather than making a spectacle of yourself with the rest of the Euro-trash."

Ouch. Although a tiny bit justified. She hadn't seen how truly shallow most of her friends were until she'd tried to rely on them as she dealt with everything—not least of which was this utterly directionless feeling of not knowing who she was or where she was going. Her friends had coaxed her to drink her way out of her funk. Something she'd briefly been led into before realizing how quickly she could turn into her father. That had scared her back onto the straight and narrow, but she couldn't believe Nic's attitude toward her bad turn after all she'd told him.

"I had to go somewhere when I was kicked out of residence. I wasn't ready to face this empty house so I stayed with friends. Where else was I supposed to go? To you, *big brother*?"

The warning that flashed in his icy blue eyes spoke of retribution for that label. She took notice, clamping her teeth together and leaning back an inch, not willing to get into a kissing contest again.

His nod was barely perceptible, but it was there, approving of her smart and hasty retreat. That irritated her. She didn't want to be afraid of him and she wasn't. She was afraid of herself and how weak he made her feel.

Sitting straighter, she said defensively, "Perhaps it wasn't the best coping strategy, but I had a lot to deal with."

"It's always about *you*, isn't it, Rowan?" Nic stood and took his time turning over the end on the surgical tape before setting it aside.

Rowan clamped shut the mouth that had dropped open. Had he not just seen with his own eyes how thoroughly she'd been living her mother's life? Fueled by righteousness, she rose hastily—then lost some of her dignity as she had to grapple for her towel. Every point on her body twinged, making her wince.

She braced herself on the wall and demanded, "You really see me as nothing more than a total narcissist, don't you?" It was so unfair.

His eyelids came down to a circumspect half-mast as he pointed out flatly, "Well, you just *had* to have a week in St. Moritz for your birthday last year, didn't you?"

Because she hadn't had the courage to come home and risk facing him after the fiasco the year before—which only added to the colossal self-blame eating her alive.

"And my broken leg put my mother and your father on the plane. Is the storm my fault too?" she asked through lips that were going numb. "Should I have checked the weather on the Med before I let that drunken snowboarder mow me down?"

Nic heard the tortured regret in her tone and recognized it as sincere, but the shriveled, underfed raisin where his heart was supposed to be didn't want to soften toward her. He couldn't afford to let it soften at all. That way led to madness and pain.

He turned away from her, and the tumult she was inciting inside him. His version of Rowan as an immature egocentric needed to stand firm against this more complex vision that was emerging, otherwise he'd be forced to re-examine himself, her, and everything that had transpired between them since day one.

"You think I don't hate myself every day?" Rowan said with a rasp that made him flinch. "Why do you think I refuse to accept they're gone? Maybe you're right, and I do need to show responsibility, but I don't want to be responsible for their being *dead*, Nic!"

A barbed hook seemed to catch at the flesh surrounding his heart.

"Olief made the decision to fly despite the weather," he muttered, unable to stand the weight of guilt she was carrying. "It's not your fault."

"No?" Her thready need for reassurance pulled at him, along with the misery searching for forgiveness in her gaze as he caught her reflection in the mirror.

"No," he affirmed, caving briefly to her palpable anguish. "You'll need your things," he added, seizing the excuse to escape the close atmosphere of the humid room. He needed to get away from her before his barriers against her crumbled any more.

It wasn't until he was halfway down the stairs that he remembered he'd had every intention of forcing Rowan to get out as soon as possible, not help her settle in.

Rowan pulled on leggings and a loose T-shirt from her closet, trying to process the consoling remark Nic had made about Olief choosing to fly. Before she could make sense of it Nic was pushing back into her room and setting her bags on the floor. He straightened and gave her a cursory, masculine once over that made her tingle.

"Let's be clear. This isn't your all-inclusive. I'll give you a few days to gather your belongings, but then you'll move on. While you're here you'll pull your weight with cooking, cleaning and laundry."

She turned her back on him to hide the sting of his sudden return to Lord of the Manor disdain. Without saying anything, she took her time twisting her wet hair into a coil and fixing it with a pair of chopsticks off her dresser-top.

"I came for the anniversary," she informed him stiffly, her insides fluttering with sexual awareness as she considered sharing this house with him. Alone. It could be unpleasant, but she wouldn't be scared off. "Don't even try to pry me out of here before then. I'll shred you to pieces."

His brows lifted and she almost heard his unspoken, *I'd like to see you try.*

Her bravado teetered as she realized he was more than big enough to physically throw her out, and had financial strength on his side, as well. For all her show of defiance, she was fragile as hell at her core. That was why she'd come back to the one constant in her life: Rosedale. She needed a sense of security while she figured out what to do.

"This is the only real home I've ever had, Nic. Maybe you and I aren't related, but this is where we gathered as a family. I need that right now." She kept her tone as steady as possible, refusing to descend into begging. "You can give me that much."

Nic braced an arm against the doorjamb, shaking his head at his bare feet before he lifted his derisive gaze. "I have to question that kind of sentimentality. What do you gain by being here for a day that has no more meaning than any other? They're gone." He wasn't being unkind, just honest—which was more difficult to face. "They're not any more or less gone whether you're here or in London or Antarctica."

Rowan gripped her elbows as she turned, shoulders hunching protectively as she absorbed what a truly unfeeling man he was. "I find it comforting to be here," she excused, hearing the creak in her voice at admitting to what he obviously saw as weakness. "But you can go back to Athens, or wherever you're living these days."

A slow smile crept across his features, completely without amusement. "You wish. No, I'll stay. And I'll even let you stay until the anniversary if you promise to sign your name on the dotted line once you've finished lighting candles in the windows."

"Why do you have to be so disparaging about it?"

"I'm being magnanimous," he defended, straightening

into cool civility. "Would you rather I make your stay conditional on your signing right now?"

"Oh, very nice," she said, instantly spitting venom over that sleight of hand. "I knew you were tough, Nic. I didn't know you were ruthless."

"Now you do," he said without acrimony.

"And you expect me to housemaid while I'm here?" Her fists dug into her ribs beneath the pressure of her elbows. "You know it was the evil step*mother* who had Cinderella scrubbing floors and sorting ballgowns all day."

"What would you rather do to earn your keep?" he shot back, swift and lethal. "Demonstrate more of your mother's survival skills?"

"Sleep with you, you mean? Not in this lifetime. Get over yourself!"

His brows shot up and his stance altered subtly to a predatory one full of challenge. Their kiss and her undeniable response was suddenly right here in the room with them. Sexual awareness gathered and sparked. The sheer magnitude of what was being acknowledged, her inability to ignore it, made Rowan's heart race in frightened anticipation. All she could think was, *Oh, my God. Oh, my God. Oh, my God*.

"It wasn't like that with Mum and Olief," she stammered. "She loved him."

"Give it a rest, Ro. I've had mistresses. I know what it's like." His chilly assessment of her figure left a trail of heat over her breasts, down her stomach and up between her thighs. "*Quid pro quo*," he said with a curl of his lip. "Not love."

His words wrenched at a place between her throat and heart. She didn't examine the source too closely. Part of it had to do with acknowledging all those unknown women who had shared his bed—something she'd never let herself think about too much—but there was a deeper sense of loss in hearing his derision of love.

"Well, I'm not going to have sex with you to stay here," she said, forcing herself to stand up to him even though she was on very shaky legs. Figuratively and literally. Despite his horrid lecture two years ago, she knew not to get into dicey situations with men and this was one of them. Best to get the *no* stated clearly. "I'm not going to let you seduce me into signing those papers before I'm good and ready either."

Her futile training in Paris for once bore fruit, allowing her to walk out gracefully on ravaged feet, her bearing straight and her shoulders proud.

CHAPTER FOUR

SEDUCE her. It was a challenge no red-blooded man could dismiss, even one whose conscience was as tortured by the prospect as his libido.

Even with the memory of Olief's setdown replaying in his mind, Nic couldn't stop fantasizing about having Rowan. She had essentially agreed to sign the papers after the anniversary, so he didn't need to try persuading her that way, but a carnal voice inside still urged him to seduce her for personal vindication. She deserved some payback for that stunt with Olief, the licentious appetite in him rationalized, not to mention a taste of the wanting and not having that he'd been suffering all these years.

Hellfire, he wanted to end this craving, but as much as he dreamed of taking her to the brink and walking away, he knew if he started something he would finish it.

That was where his hard-earned self-protective instincts kicked in and reminded him not to do anything rash. If you played with fire you got burned, and there was definitely a fire in that woman. Their kiss, the way her mouth had opened and crushed into the pressure of his, wouldn't leave his mind, making him useless behind his desk.

Given that his plans had changed, and he'd now be here a full two weeks, he had spent the afternoon reconfiguring Olief's office space to his own taste so he could work more productively. It wasn't happening. Despite Rosedale being big and quiet, he was intensely aware there was another occupant here.

Forget her, he commanded himself. But there were other distractions. The promised thunderstorm had brought darkness early and was rattling the windows. Hunger gnawed at his belly, reminding him he'd skipped lunch. He needed to approve this project and get it back to the VP while the time change window was still open, though.

Another flash of lightning bleached the windows and a huge clap of thunder reverberated above the house. The lights flickered—then everything went black.

Nic swore at the inconvenience. The wiring here was modern and top-notch. All the equipment was protected with surge bars. The vineyard manager would investigate the outage and report it. All he'd lost was his wi-fi connection and the widescreen monitor. A glance at his laptop in its dock showed the battery light gleaming reliably. Nic opened the lid and the screen came alive with a pallid glow. He flicked his mobile into hotspot mode and was able to retrieve his report and continue making comments.

"Nic?" The flickering yellow of a candle entered the room ahead of Rowan, her face sweetly tinted with warm golden light.

The words *seduce her* tantalized him again. He sat back, thinking, *Do it because you want to*. Such a bad idea.

"Afraid of the thunder?" he taunted lightly.

She set the squat candle in its round bowl on the corner of his desk. "I thought you might be fumbling around in the dark, but of course you're perfectly equipped."

"Thanks for noticing," he drawled, and wondered if that was a blush climbing into her shadowed cheeks or just the flush of impatience women got when a man made an off-color remark. "I'm fine. Working without interruption, in fact." He turned his nose back to the screen to steer himself from temptation.

He still tracked Rowan as she took an idle stroll into the dark corners of the office, pausing at the window as rain gusted against the glass before taking herself to the bookshelf of worn style-guides, atlases, and other reference tomes.

"Use my tablet if you want a novel," he offered. "There are hundreds on it."

"If I have time to read, I have time to practice." She said it like something she'd memorized by rote. "Same goes for television—not that that's an option right now." She came away from the bookshelf with a look that was both disgruntled and lost. "I've already done my exercises. If I work my leg anymore I'll just hurt myself. I was about to start dinner, but the freezer is empty and the power's gone."

"I brought the boat," Nic reminded her, his body involuntarily reacting to the way she moved like a leaf in a stream, meandering in a way that mesmerized him.

"I've had enough of the sea today, thanks." Her aimless path took her to a lamp fringe, which she lightly stroked, making the silk lift and fall in a ripple.

This was so like her—the way she accepted as her due that a room would pause and take notice when she entered. What was it about her that made it happen? he wondered. She was lovely, with her buttermilk skin and sable hair, the sensual softness of her features and the toned perfection of her frame, but that wasn't what gave her such power. There was something more innate, something warm, that promised happiness and fulfillment if she noticed you.

Nic shut down that bizarre tangent of thought. He was not one of those people who fell for charisma, watching and waiting for the next act, aching to feel important because he was touched by her attention.

Irritated with himself, he did what he'd always done when Rowan inveigled herself into his space. He pretended he was ignoring her even though he could practically feel the heat off her body from across the room.

That was his libido keeping her on its scope. He hadn't made much time for women in the last year and his body was noticing.

"Cold sandwiches are fine," he said. "Bring mine here so I can keep working."

"That reminds me. I should have said earlier, Nic." She moved toward him, pale fingers coming to rest like a pianist's on the opposite edge of his desk. The candlelight made her solemn expression all the more wide-eyed and impactful. "What you've done for Olief? Looking after things for him? That's good of you. I'm sure he'd appreciate it."

The unexpected praise turned him inside out. No one had ever suggested he was a good son. Olief certainly hadn't acknowledged him that way—ever—and Nic had long given up expecting him to. Having Rowan offer this shred of recognition was a surprise stiletto through the ribs that slid past his barriers to prick at the most deeply protected part of himself.

For a second he couldn't breathe. The sensation was so real and sharp and paralyzing. Then his inner SWAT team snapped into action and he remembered her using this same gamine face and earnest charm to garner affectionate pats on the head and indulgent approval from Olief. They'd been president of each other's fan club, and now she was obviously looking for a new partner in her mutual admiration society.

"I'm not doing it for him," Nic stated bluntly, angry with himself for sucking up her flattery like a dry sponge.

"But…" Rowan's brows came together and she took

a half step back from the refutation she read in his face. "Who, then?"

"Myself. I've been working my way up since he brought me aboard to launch his web journals on the Middle East ten years ago. It was a merger, actually, since I was already established in the electronic publishing side. I made it clear then that I had ambitions. He hadn't named me as heir, and I wasn't at the top of his corporate succession plan when he disappeared, but it was due to be reviewed and we both knew this is where I wanted to end up."

"What do you mean, he didn't…? Of *course* you're his heir!"

Rowan's certainty made a harsh bubble of laughter rise to catch in Nic's throat. They were talking about a man who hadn't spoken to his son until Nic had walked up to him at an awards gala and said, "*I believe you knew my mother.*"

With fresh rancor, Nic said, "We won't know who inherits until he's been declared dead and his will is read. Perhaps he left his fortune to Cassandra and you?"

With a shake of her head that made loose tendrils of hair catch the candlelight and glitter like an angel's halo, Rowan said, "You're his son. And you can build on what he's already accomplished. Of course he would leave everything to you. Except maybe Rosedale." Her chin hitched with challenge as she gave him a considering look.

"This land was bought as an investment property to be developed. It's never been taken off the books as a company asset," Nic said. "I know that much."

"Therefore you control it as long as you're in that chair?"

"Exactly."

Her narrow shoulders slid a notch, but her breasts lost none of their thrust. For a skinny little thing, she had beautifully rounded breasts. All of her was a little curvier than he remembered. It was nice. Healthy.

"If I *did* inherit everything from Olief, I could fire you."

Her disdainful look down her nose was the kind of entitled sassiness that had always made him want to yank her off her self-built pedestal. He reminded himself not to let her engage his emotions.

"I've spent the last year proving to the board I'm the right man for the job. They're not going to switch allegiance on the whim of a spoiled brat—despite your proven ability to charm older men."

Her chin twitched at the word 'spoiled' before her thick lashes came together and her most impudent smile appeared. "Don't underestimate me. I charm the younger ones, too."

"Yes, you always manage to get what you want, don't you?" he said with chilly disgust. "Until now."

As soon as he said it a vision of her feet flashed in his mind's eye and he heard her again. *I want my family.* The source of hardness in him turned on its edge, pressing at an unpleasant angle against his lungs. He grimaced, wishing for her to be the diva ballerina he'd always found easy to dismiss.

"Am I really that bad, Nic?" Her white hands sifted the air. "Maybe Olief *did* pay my expenses, but developing as a dancer was my *job*. I didn't have time to hold down a real one. And, yes, I did take things too far in the last few months, but it was the first time I'd been free to! I kept waiting for someone to set me a limit and finally realized *I* had to. Everyone goes through that on the way to becoming an adult. You're making out like I'm all new cars and caviar, but what did I ever have that you didn't?"

His laptop timed out, abruptly going black and dimming the room into a place of darkness and shadows. Thunder continued to rumble in the distance, along with the piercing wail of wind and the churn of rough waves against the shore.

"What a loaded question," he muttered, stabbing a key to make the screen come back to life, and rising restlessly at the same time. "What did you have?" he repeated.

He rounded his desk to confront her in the cold bluish glow. He couldn't contain the confused hurt bottled against the spurned rock that was his heart.

"Do you have any idea what it's like to meet your father for the first time when you're an adult? To finally be invited into his home only to watch him fawn over the daughter of his mistress—a girl who isn't even related to him—while knowing he never once wasted affection on his *real* flesh and blood? Now, to be fair, my mother was only a one-night stand—not a long-term companion like your mother—but he knew about me from birth. He paid for my education, but he never so much as dropped by the boarding school to say hello. I came to believe he was incapable of fatherly warmth." He'd had to. It had been the only way to cope. "Then I saw him with you."

Rowan drew in a breath that seemed to shrink her lungs, making her insides feel small and tense. Olief was the one safe, reliable, loving person she could go to without being told to try harder, commit deeper, be better. That was why his disappearance was killing her. She missed him horribly. She loved him.

And apparently Nic felt she'd stolen all those precious moments at *his* expense.

"At least that explains why you hate me." Nic, like everyone, had expected better of her and, like always, she didn't know how she could have been different. All she could do was what she'd always done: apologize. "I'm sorry. I never meant to get between you."

"Didn't you?" he shot back, his feral energy expanding until her skin prickled with goose bumps.

She felt caught red-handed. Her old crush on him sputtered to life in neon glory, making her feel gauche. The memory of today's kiss, which she'd managed to ignore through sheer force of will since entering this room, was released like an illicit drug in her mind—one that stole her ability to think and expanded her physical perceptions.

Betraying heat flooded into her loins while the tips of her breasts tightened. She was hyper-aware of his male power held in tight restraint. For years he'd looked at her with bored aversion. Today he was seeing her, and his gaze was full of the force of his primal nature, accusatory and personal.

And for once she understood his animosity.

The defusing explanation didn't come easily. Her throat didn't want to let the words out. They were too revealing.

"I know I often interrupted the two of you. Please don't judge me too harshly for that." She had wanted so badly to catch Nic's attention. Being in his presence had made her heart sing—not unlike right now, she thought in an uncomfortable aside, burning on a pyre of self-conscious embarrassment. "I wanted to hear your stories," she excused, trying to downplay what a wicked pleasure it had been to eavesdrop on his rumbling voice. His analytical intelligence with such an underlying thirst for justice had drawn her irresistibly. Her fingers tangled together in front of her. "You were traveling the world while I couldn't steal time to climb the Eiffel Tower in my own backyard. Don't fault me for wanting to live your adventures."

"Adventures? I was reporting on civil wars! Crimes against humanity! Those sorts of tales aren't fit for a woman's ears, let alone the child you were then. The only reason I brought them up with Olief was because he'd been there. He understood the line that has to be drawn between exposing the horrors and scaring the hell out of people. You can't do that kind of work without unloading somewhere."

Rowan was struck by more than his words. His eyes darkened and his expression flashed with a suffering that he quickly shuttered away. Her view of his work had always been that it was genuinely glamorous and important, not just appearing that way like her own. His face was splashed on magazine covers, wasn't it? He was no stranger to being a still, compelling presence before a camera. He had accolades galore for his efforts.

There was a toll for bringing forth the stories that held an audience rapt, though. Perhaps she *was* horribly self-involved, since she'd never considered what sorts of anguish and cruelty he'd witnessed in getting those stories. He would have pushed himself because he was a man of ambition, but his opinion pieces revealed a man who wanted to restore peace and justice. That wasn't work for the faint-hearted. If he was tough and closed off it was because he had to be in order to get what he wanted for the betterment of humanity.

Everything in her longed to surge forward and somehow offer comfort, but his body language—shoulders bunched, head turned to the side—shouted *back off*.

She stared down at bare feet that were icy despite the carpet she stood on.

"I always wondered why you were always so…" Aloof? Emotionless? Haunted? "Quiet."

She rubbed her arms, trying to bring life back into herself when she felt chilled to the bone. Her heart ached for him. Of course he would have needed someone to help put all those terrible sights into perspective. She wanted to scroll back time and watch from afar, allowing him the healing he'd so obviously needed.

"I wish you'd said something," she said weakly. "I wouldn't have got in your way with Olief if I'd known how bad it was."

"No?" he challenged, with another shot of that searing aggression.

"Of course not! I'm not so self-centered that I felt threatened by your having a relationship with your own father."

"Then why did you set it up for him to see us on the beach and take a strip off me for it? That was a depth of bitchiness that exceeded even *my* low expectations of you, Ro." His recrimination made her knees go weak.

The tiny thread of hope she'd found and clasped on to, the tentative belief that she was making headway with understanding Nic's reserve and softening his judgment of her, snapped like a rubber band, not only stealing her optimism with a sharp sting, but launching her into an empty space where there was only hard landings.

"Olief *saw* that?" The one person who liked her exactly as she was had seen her inept plea to be noticed and the humiliating rejection that had followed. Rowan wanted to sink through the carpet and disappear. She dropped her cringing face into her hands.

"Oh, give it a rest. The awards committee isn't in residence," Nic bit out.

"I passed Olief on the path, but I didn't think he'd seen us!" She only lifted her mortified face because she was determined to make him believe her. "Do you honestly think I'd want anyone to know I behaved so cheaply? I can hardly face *you*."

"Then why did you do it?" His eyes were cold and measuring, unwilling to accept her protest at face value. "It better be good, Rowan, because he made me feel like a pervert, saying men like me had no business with a girl like you. What the hell does *that* mean? *Men like me?* Too old? Or simply not good enough? Forget finding common ground after that. We were barely speaking."

Her throat closed again. She felt sick with herself. She had to 'fess up or he'd believe forever that she was a tease, and worse—someone who had schemed to hurt him for no reason but a power trip. She couldn't live with that. She wasn't like that at all.

"I…I wanted to," she managed in a strangled whisper, furnace-like heat unleashing in her to conflagrate her whole body. She felt like the candle flame swaying on its spineless wick, all her dignity melting into a transparent puddle beneath her.

"Wanted to what?" he demanded. "Make me look like an opportunist?"

"No!" Rowan pitied every minion who'd ever had to stand before him and explain herself. He was utterly formidable. But his demeanor was the kind of unyielding superciliousness she'd been knuckling under all her life. She was *so* tired of apologizing for being human and having flaws!

"I wanted to kiss you," she blurted with defiance, staring him right in the eye while every nerve-ending fried under the responding flash of heat in his gaze. "I was attracted to you. We all have urges," she excused with a shrug, desperate to play it down so he wouldn't know *how* attracted. "I'd had a few drinks. It seemed like a good idea."

For a long time he only stared at her, while the silence played out and the shadows closed in. Just as she began to feel sweat popping across her upper lip he moved closer, studying her so intently her skin tightened all over her body.

"You wanted a kiss bad enough to chase me to the beach for it?"

"Take your pound of flesh if you need it. Yes, I chased you and, yes, I realize how desperate that makes me seem.

It was an impulse. I didn't get out much and it was my birthday." If she kept slapping coats of whitewash on it perhaps he wouldn't see it for the act of lifelong yearning it had been.

"All those years of batting your lashes and trying to get a rise out of me… It wasn't more of that same nonsense?"

She had to drop her gaze then, because it had very much been a culmination of that long, infernal effort to catch his interest.

His hand came under her jaw, forcing her chin up so she couldn't hide from his penetrating glacier-blue eyes. "Because I can forgive a teenager for baiting a grown man, but at twenty you should have known better."

"So you said then, and I wasn't doing that." Impatience got the better of her and she tried to pull away, dying inside as she recalled his angry kiss and his merciless rejection.

His hand moved to the side of her neck, long fingers sliding beneath the fall of her hair so his fingertips rested on the back of her neck, keeping her close.

"And today?" he asked, his tone dangerously lethal.

"Today you kissed *me*." It took guts to hold her ground, especially when she was flushed with self-disgust as she recalled how she'd reacted: as if she still thought kissing him was a good idea. Her nails cut into her palms as she made herself face him and the crushing truth. "Or rather you tried to manipulate me with what mechanically resembled a kiss."

He gave a little snort. "I'm long past the age of playing games. It was more than mechanics. We kissed each other."

He made it sound like something to be savored. When he dropped his gaze to her mouth her stomach tightened. Her whole body tingled and her lips began to burn.

"We started something two years ago that wants finishing."

Her hand came up instinctively to the middle of his chest. He hadn't moved any closer, but she suddenly felt threatened. Her arteries swelled as all her blood began to move harder and faster. "Wh-what do you mean?"

"I'm not blind, Rowan." He glanced down to where her still-bandaged hand pressed against his chest. His strong heartbeat pounded into her palm. "I noticed in the last few years that you weren't a kid anymore. The only thing that stopped me taking what you were offering that night was a certainty that you didn't mean it. If you had…"

She sucked in a breath and jerked back, pulling her hand into her breasts as though his glance at her knuckles had branded them.

Nic folded his arms across his chest, his shoulders hardening. "*Did* you mean it?" he demanded. "Are we finally being honest or still playing games?"

This was moving too fast. "I'm not going to sleep with you, Nic!"

"Because you still want to tie me up in knots for kicks?"

Was he feeling tied up? Insidious heat flooded into her pelvis, licking with wanton anticipation at her insides. He couldn't be serious. She told her feet to run, but they refused. "We can't have some kind of fling and then carry on as if…"

She trailed off, the little cogs in her head making hard, sharp connections that stuck long enough to reverberate painfully in her skull before clicking over to the next one as she took in the way Nic's brows lifted in aloof inquisition.

She was a virgin, not sophisticated and experienced enough to have flings. Nic *was* experienced, though, and when he had flings he carried on just fine afterward because he never saw his partner again. Which was exactly what he intended with Rowan.

How had she not grasped that? He had come here intending to kick her out and never see her again. She'd won a stay of eviction, but after the two weeks were up they would not cross paths again—not unless it was by chance.

She would never see Nic again. Ever. How had she not taken that in?

Because she had subliminally believed that when she was ready she would seek him out. Never once had she thought there would be no Rosedale to come back to—no Nic prowling the grounds where she could put herself under his nose with only minimal risk and wait for him to notice her.

The gray void that was her future grew bigger and more desolate.

"As if what?" he prompted.

She gave a dry laugh, using it to cover the damp thickness gathering in her throat. "I naively thought an affair could make for awkward Christmas dinners in future, but that won't be a problem, will it? I really am saying goodbye to everything I knew and—"

Don't say it. Rowan swallowed and twisted her hands together, trying to rub sensation into fingers that were going numb. "I wish you had some feeling of having a home and family here, Nic. I really do. I'll make us some sandwiches."

She picked up the candle and walked out, leaving him in the glow of the laptop. She didn't see how he stood in the same place long after the device timed out again, silent and alone in the dark.

CHAPTER FIVE

Nic was still letting Rowan's remark eat at him the next morning, and he couldn't fathom why. It wasn't as if he hadn't heard variations of it from other women.

He had concluded over the years that there was a deficiency in him that portrayed him as not needing what others did: a home, family, love. And since he had been denied those things all his life he had learned to live without them. He *didn't* need them. It was a closed loop.

So why did he feel so unfairly judged by Rowan's, *I wish you had some feeling of having a home and family here*? Even if he wanted to be different, he couldn't. The thought of trying to change made his hands curl into fists and a current of nervousness pulse through his system.

"I'm going for groceries!" she shouted from the bottom floor, startling him from his introspection.

Good, he thought, needing a reprieve from the way she upset his equilibrium. "Check the car insurance," he responded in a yell.

"Okay. Bye!"

He let out a sigh, forcing himself back to his desk and the work spread over it, dimly aware of the distant hum of the garage door and then the growl of a motor—

She wouldn't.

Leaping to his feet, he shot open the window in time

to see his vintage black convertible, top down, slithering with the speed of a hungry mamba up the curving drive. Tucking fingertip and thumb against his teeth, he pierced the air with a furious whistle.

The brake lights came on. Her glossy head turned to look back at the house.

Nic pointed at the front steps and met her there a few seconds later. Rowan chirped the brakes as she stopped before him, staying behind the wheel while all eight cylinders purred. Glamorous Tiffany sunglasses obscured half her face, but her mouth trembled in a subtle betrayal of nervousness before she sat a little straighter and gave him a lady-of-the-manor, "Yes?"

"What the hell are you doing?" He hitched his elbow on the top of the windscreen from the passenger side.

"You said to check the insurance. This one is still valid."

"So is the hatchback."

"This is more fun." She pulled out one of her cheeky grins, trying to cajole him into indulging her.

He narrowed his eyes, determined not to fall for her act the way the rest of his sex did. "And you know that *how*?"

Her nose crinkled. "I *might* have taken Black Betty here for a spin once or twice before. But I always fill the tank." The assertive finger she lifted fell. "Today that could be a problem, though. I took the petty cash from the kitchen, but it wasn't much."

"You are utterly shameless, aren't you? I'm speechless." Unaccountably, he had to suppress an urge to laugh.

"Okay. Well, could you…um…step back while you ponder what you'd like to say?"

"Get out of my car, Rowan!"

"Oh, Nic, don't be like that," she coaxed, leaning toward him so the chunky zipper of her flight jacket gaped open and showed him the line of her dark plum scooped-shirt plastered low across her breasts. Pale globes swelled over the top.

"Like what?" He tried not to get distracted. "I know you. You'll start looking at a basket of puppies and won't notice the rain's started again."

But was he any different? A monsoon could blow in at this moment and he'd still be fascinated by *those* puppies.

She caught him looking. He wasn't exactly being discreet, so it wasn't a surprise to lift his gaze and find a smug grin of womanly power widening her lips. In the way of all beauties who recognized the advantage of their appeal, she assumed it was legal tender.

"I'll put the top up at the first spit, I promise." She slipped the car into gear.

He shook his head, as much at himself for revealing his weakness as at her for thinking she had him where she wanted him. "No."

"Look at this gorgeous morning." She gestured expansively at the broken clouds scudding across the brilliant blue sky. Streaks of sunlight bathed the rainwashed landscape in pockets of gold. "Doesn't it make you want to feel the sun on your face and the wind in your hair?"

He never allowed himself to be susceptible to Rowan's appealing enthusiasm. Old reflexes crowded a refusal onto his tongue. *Park the convertible and use the hatchback. I have to work.* Work was the one thing he did care about. It was always there and, since it was all he would ever have, he was making a legacy of it.

But a damp sweet breeze floated across his face, hinting at spring. It turned his mind to the instinctive pursuits of the season—the mating season. His blood warmed with male appreciation of the youthful female smiling up at him with such guile.

Seduce her. The words whispered on the air.

At the very least he should remind her that batting her lashes had consequences.

"Give me the keys," he said on impulse.

"Oh, Nic!" Rowan cut the engine and flung open the driver's door. As he came around to her side, a long thigh in tight green jeans stretched out. Tall boots were planted with firm temper. "Why do you have to be like this? You're just like everyone else who thinks they own my life. '*No, Rowan, you can't possibly have five minutes of enjoying yourself. Take the housekeeper's hatchback because that's what you are now.*' What do you gain from these power trips, huh, Nic? What?"

She stood before him in the V of the open door. The full impact of her tough, piqued magnificence hit him like a truck. He'd thought to play her at her own game, but the stakes were high. It took everything he had to hold out a steady hand.

"I get to drive. Are you going to stand there and sulk or move to the other seat?"

"You're coming with me? To the market?"

Her stunned surprise was mostly hidden by her sunglasses, but he got to watch her elegant chin drop and her glossy lips part. The urge to kiss her edged him into her space.

"Wouldn't you like company? I have my wallet." He felt for it.

She shook back her hair, taking a second to eye him warily. If he hadn't felt the weak sunshine before, he got a full blast of fireball heat as they stood facing each other. The attraction built in exponential waves of silence, bouncing back and forth, compressing with super-nova potential for explosion. Excitement for the chase swelled in him like a wind catching a sail.

"Of course."

Her winning smile was meant to disarm and it did.

His abdomen tightened, but when she made an abbreviated move to slip around him he stayed exactly where he was. He wanted her to brush up against him.

The barest hint of nervousness diluted her bravado before she stated airily, "I guess I'll crawl through."

She planted her knee in the driver's seat and offered him a breathtaking view of her wiggling backside while she maneuvered into the passenger seat. Righting herself, she inquired sweetly, "Will you be warm enough without a jacket?"

"Plenty," he drawled, his jeans feeling as snug as hers were. This was insane. "The market and back," he stated as he dropped behind the wheel. "I have a corporation to run."

"I know, and I appreciate you doing this."

Her hand grazed his bare wrist as he turned the key. All the hair stood up on his arm.

"I want us to be friends, Nic."

His insides turned over with the engine. She had to be kidding. Dislodging her touch, he reached across to steal her sunglasses so he could see her as clearly as she saw him. He wanted to watch her comprehend that they'd come too far for any more pretense.

"The extent of the attraction between us doesn't seem to be penetrating for you. We'll never be friends, Ro. People with this much sexual desire between them can't be."

The undisguised stare of masculine intent from Nic started a pull in her belly. Rowan resisted it with a clench of her stomach muscles. Through a night of tossing and turning she'd absorbed that Nic didn't keep his lovers in his life. He was ruthlessly throwing her out of her home. She absolutely shouldn't have an affair with him. But here she was, unable to resist flirting with him when she could see, at last, that she had an effect on him. Insidious thoughts crept in that she might be able to persuade him against his plans for Rosedale if she got close enough to him.

Being close was heady, but frightening. She'd grasped at the let's-be-friends routine to slow things down. He wasn't having it, and the sexual energy between them couldn't be ignored when they were crammed together in this tiny car, her sunglasses dangling from his fingers behind her head. He was caressing her face with his gaze, taking in the telltale bags under her eyes that she'd tried to cover with makeup. She couldn't help dropping her gaze to his mouth and recalling the way those lips had hardened against hers, feasting and appreciating.

The lips in question curled into a knowing smile.

"I—" She became aware of a slow burn inside her, like a fuse that had been lit and was taking its time creeping toward the cache of gunpowder.

"I want you, Rowan." Her sunglasses slid down her shoulder into her lap as his fingers combed her hair over her ear. "I've wanted you for a long time. And knowing you want me too means I have no reason to keep my distance any longer. It's only a matter of time before we satisfy our curiosity."

"Curiosity?" she repeated, her heart trip-hammering as she processed that he'd wanted her for a long time. "You make it sound so…" *Unemotional.* Of course it was pure physical desire for him. It still managed to pierce her with a sweet shot of excitement.

Blinking to ease the sting in her eyes, she shrugged, fighting the urge to turn her lips into his wrist, where his warm hand cupped the side of her head. God help her if she revealed she was motivated by something far more tender than basic earthly appetites.

As a bit of self-protection, she murmured, "You make it sound like you just want to get to the bottom of this."

She waited a beat before she gave him the limpid, *ingénue* blink that would tell him she knew exactly what a *double-entendre* she'd just delivered.

It only took a stunned second before he tipped back his head in a hearty laugh—a rare full-bodied sound that melted her heart. *Thanks, Mum*, she thought with a caustic nod of acknowldgement to the woman who'd taught her the valuable art of flirting. Cassandra had always used it aggressively, to bring a man in line with her wants, whereas Rowan wielded it for defense. But at least it was in her repertoire of skills.

"Well, it would go a long way to easing the tension between us, wouldn't it?" Nic mused as he released her to gun the engine and pull away.

The wind whipped Rowan's hair into her eyes. She slouched into the sheepskin collar of her jacket, but it was more like sinking into the miasma of thrilling emotions filling her. Nic wanted her.

It shouldn't make her tremble like she was six and it was Christmas morning—not when it came with warnings of painful consequences—but all her sexual awareness as a woman was wrapped up in this man. Her adolescent hormones had first been stirred by his solitary masculine figure striding from the surf. As she had matured all her searches for a mate had been a search for Nic's attributes in another man. Of all the kisses she'd experienced none had been topped by the brief, savage touch of Nic's lips on the beach that night two years ago.

Until yesterday.

Peeling a tendril of hair from her eyes, she replaced her sunglasses and then found Nic's in the glove box. He slid them on with the silently efficient way he did everything else. Adeptly. With confidence. With a proprietorial attitude as if he owned the road, knew each curve and how to manipulate it.

Good grief, he didn't have to seduce her. She was doing it for him!

It must be the pending anniversary, she concluded with pensive insight. She'd always had a crush on Nic, but her emotions were exaggerated right now, making her more sensitive and quick to react to any offer of intimacy. She was moving into a state of closure, one that was going to have many fronts if Nic really did expel her from Rosedale and tear it down. Her entire life was being compressed and squeezed through the eye of a needle. Hardly anything of the old life would come with her. Out of desperation she was reaching for anything and everything to hang on to, including Nic.

Especially Nic.

A stuttering sigh ripped through her chest, hidden by the drone of the engine and the rush of the wind. She glanced at him to see if he was tracking her inner struggle.

He kept his attention on the road, his profile starkly beautiful in its intensity, his cheeks still shiny from his morning shave, his mouth the only thing about him that seemed to relax. She longed to trace his mouth with her fingertips.

Maybe she needed to give herself to him in order to get over him once and for all.

Her stomach swooped and her head grew light. The thought of sex with him scared the hell out of her, but her shudder wasn't all trepidation. It was also a delicious betrayal of anticipation. She wanted him.

She forced her hands to uncurl on her thighs, aware that she was kidding herself if she thought sleeping with him would help her get over him. She wanted to go to bed with Nic because deep down she thought maybe, somehow, it would make him *like* her. All night she had tossed and turned, tormented by the mistakes she'd made that had led him to look down on her. She wanted to make up with him. Sleep with him. He was the only man she'd ever wanted to sleep with. That was what it came down to.

But she was a virgin.

And he didn't want anything from the experience but to satisfy his curiosity. He wanted to rock her world and then drop out of it.

Those rather pertinent details filled her with serious misgivings about sliding into bed with him. What would he say? Would it be good? Or awkward and disappointing? Would they be able to part with a sense of closure? Or would it be relief on his side and a mortifying memory for her that tortured her forever?

Would he even want her? Or would he lose interest once he realized she wasn't a sex symbol like her mother?

The fluttering tents of the outdoor market came into view. Nic pulled into the parking lot that was always crowded in the middle of summer, but sparsely occupied today. They drew attention—not just because of the flashy car and the quiet time of year, but because locals knew who they were. It made for a poignant hour of shopping as they fielded questions about the called-off search.

Her Greek was passable, Nic's impeccable, so she let him talk even though what he said took her aback.

"No, we're not planning anything except a follow-up retrospective in select publications and international programs."

Rowan had come to Rosedale thinking to mark the anniversary privately, but if the plan was now to put a final stamp of acceptance on their loss something more definitive was needed: a memorial service and a proper laying to rest.

She was about to bring it up with Nic, but he turned and pressed his hand to the middle of her back, steering her toward the pastry stall. It was a fairly innocuous bit of handling, but she felt as though his chilled fingers reached through the layers of leather and fabric to caress her bare spine. All thought left her beyond an awareness of the cottony scent of his shirt and the muskier warmth near his throat.

He glanced down to see why she'd frozen in her tracks and a moment of electrified tension grew around them like a force field. Nic didn't move, but he seemed to grow bigger, becoming more intimidating and more of a threat to her self-possession. Her heart started to pound hard in her chest. He was only being Nic—sex-god with a hot physique and a way of looking at her as though he knew exactly how completely her senses came alive the second she was near him.

"You're getting curious about me," he accused in a husky scold.

She couldn't help it, despite her qualms. Her palms grew damp and she lowered her gaze to the nearly invisible golden hairs lying flat against the warm skin of his chest where it was exposed by his open collar.

This was a disconcerting experience, being pursued and wanting back. Saying no had always been easy because she had never felt drawn to the men who propositioned her. Suddenly she was susceptible to her own inner weakness and that scared her.

"There's curiosity and there's high-risk behavior," she managed to toss out, retreating a hasty step as a nervous lump formed in her throat. "I'm actually quite choosy. More than you, if the rotation of women on your arm is anything to go by." She kept her tone slightly jaded so he wouldn't guess how genuinely put out and intimidated she was by the extent of his experience.

As she pretended to deliberate between French éclairs and honey-soaked baklava, he came up behind her and requested, "Two of each," from the heavyset baker.

Rowan never allowed herself those sorts of treats, but she couldn't contradict him. Her whole body was paralyzed by the brush of his body against hers.

He waited until the plump woman turned away before saying quietly in English, "And yet I keep getting the impression you've chosen me."

Her knees nearly unhinged. It was too fast, too much of an assumption.

"My hormones might have, but I've given up more than just alcohol and parties. I didn't like not being in control of myself—"

Big mistake. He leaned forward to exchange a few bills for the box of pastries and cut her an eloquent look rife with the anticipation of a challenge.

Her heart took a heavy swing and a dangerous dip. "I'm trying to act like an adult rather than follow silly impulses," she defended. "That should impress you."

"This isn't an impulse. It's an inevitability." Nic couldn't help putting his hand on her again, finding the spot just above her tailbone where her jacket had ridden up.

Her buttocks tensed and a tiny shudder rippled through her before she started back toward the car. Rowan wasn't a fidgety person, but Nic was getting a distinct impression of skittishness. Was it because what she was feeling was stronger than what she thought she could control?

His mind went into a meltdown of smugness and desperation. He'd be damned if he'd admit it was the same for him, though. Part of him already felt defeated at the way he'd let things progress this far, this fast. He told himself he was playing her at her own game, but he was succumbing to exactly what he'd called it: inevitability. A tight coil of desire held him in its grip and all his focus had shifted to having her.

It was a weakness he could only bear if Rowan felt the same. If she didn't… A barbed hook caught at his chest, giving a merciless yank. To reassure himself he set his hand on her thigh once she was seated, stroking lightly to part her knees and press her to make room between her boots for the bag of groceries.

Rowan's leg jerked reflexively and she let out a subtle hiss, her eyes lifting to reveal pupils that went black as a hole in the universe.

Nic deliberately shifted his touch to a gentle caress of her knee. "Did I bump a scrape?" he asked silkily, but with genuine concern. He picked up her hand. "I see the bandages are off." He turned up her palm to see the cross-hatched skin was red and tender, but healing. "Looks better. That's good."

Rowan's fingers trembled revealingly before she quickly tugged from his grip.

"Men are so predictable," she said with an exasperated shake of her head. "You think you hear a dare and now your ego demands you prove something. I've been pressured too many times into doing things I didn't want to do. I won't let you bully me."

"Of course not," he said, oddly affected by how vulnerable she seemed all of a sudden. Beautiful, stubborn, and hesitantly anxious behind a wall of determination. A protective feeling flickered through him, but the fire was still there, always there, raging unceasingly. He let a smile touch his lips as he very gently smoothed her hair behind her ear, taking his time so they could both enjoy the quiet, deliberate caress.

A pretty flush gathered under her cheeks and her lashes fluttered with confusion while her lips seemed to bloom into a plump pout.

"Don't worry, Ro. I understand a woman's need for foreplay. I'm not going to rush you." He almost went for a kiss, but remembered how public they were.

Straightening, he let the wind slice through his shirt and cool his scalp for a moment before noticing the sky was gathering for another downpour. They might outrun it. He was certainly motivated to hurry back.

Nic's stark promise kept replaying in Rowan's head. *Foreplay.* Was that why he grazed his knuckles against her thigh as he shifted gears? And played that music with the sexy Latino beat that echoed the thick pulse of her blood and put a soundtrack in her hips?

He had almost kissed her before he'd rounded the bonnet and climbed in on the driver's side, and despite her plucky talk about holding him off all she could think about was hurtling back to Rosedale. Quiet, secure, private Rosedale. Where they might kiss.

And do more? She didn't know—literally didn't know—what to do.

He pulled up unexpectedly beneath the sprawl of a huge olive tree.

Rowan swung a wary glance at him, both relieved by the reprieve and mildly terrified that he had changed his mind about going home.

"It's starting to rain." He stepped out of the car and pulled his seat forward. "Didn't you notice?" he taunted lightly.

She had no choice then but to offer a vague look into the olive grove and murmur, "Oh, look—puppies."

"You're not funny."

"Sure I am." She left the car and pulled her own seat forward to help him retrieve the removable side windows and canvas top. Her reflexes felt clumsy as she helped him snap and button everything into place, her whole being intimidated by the easy mastery with which he moved.

The patter of rain on the budding branches above them increased as they finished, bouncing through to hit them in fat dollops. They slammed themselves back into the car as the sky opened up. The drumming became a wild rush of sound.

As the windscreen blurred with heavy rain Rowan glanced at him, expecting him to start the car and pull out. In the muted light his blue eyes were charcoal, his body a mass of gathered energy.

"What's wrong?" she asked.

"I can't wait." He leaned across, one hand cupping her cheek as he slanted his mouth in hot possession over hers.

Rowan gasped, parting her lips. Nic took devastating advantage, thrusting past the games and hesitations of their past kisses and slamming them into a new reality of raw seduction. His arm came behind her shoulders, gathering her up and providing a pillow as she yielded. So much had changed between them in the last twenty-four hours Rowan couldn't do anything but give herself over to the flood of desire.

When his tongue touched hers lust struck with blinding ferocity, lighting a fire of aggression in her that made her kiss him back with equal fervor, lashing at his tongue with her own, fueling the blaze of need expanding around them.

She was dimly aware of a soft growl in his throat, that his fingers moved in a gentle caress of her jaw and throat, but she wouldn't give up their kiss. Her hands went into his hair, holding him so she could harden the press of their mouths, inhibitions demolished by how instantaneously he inflamed her. She needed this more than air.

With another feral sound he slid his hand to her breast, boldly sliding beneath the scoop neck of her top and invading the snug cup of her bra.

At the first catch of his fingers across her nipple Rowan released a cry into his mouth, startled by the shot of intense pleasure that bolted directly into the heart of her.

Nic pulled away, watching as he exposed her breast. Rowan thought she ought to be embarrassed, but she wasn't. He wore a reverent look, like her pink nipple was beautiful, thrusting so wantonly. She couldn't help but feel pride as she basked in his ravenous gaze.

Then he lowered his head and took her into the hot velvet of his mouth. A keening sound left her. The sensation was so intense and sustained. Cradling his head in her forearms, she pressed her legs tightly together, trying to ease the ache throbbing between.

He pulled back a little, just enough to jerk open his shirt. "Touch me." He brought her hand to his hot chest, then forced his own between her clenched thighs.

Rowan splayed her hands on his hot damp skin, bombarded by too many sensations: the loving stroke of his tongue against her throat, the rasp of silky chest hair on her raw palms and the stunning pleasure that accompanied the firm cup of his hand where she wanted pressure most.

He kissed her again, short-circuiting her brain. Her hips rose into the press of his palm. She tried to feel all of him: the hair-roughened muscles of his chest, the flat quiver of his belly, the silky smoothness of his spine. As her fingertips quested toward the waistband of his jeans he pulled back again.

"Do you have anything?" His voice was deep and sensual, urgent and ragged.

"What—?" She was so new to this it took a second for her to understand. "Protection, you mean? No!"

"You're not on the Pill?"

"No!"

With a soft curse he fell back in his seat, hands gripping the wheel so hard his knuckles turned white. "That's probably for the best. This car is impossible. What would we do? Lie down in the grass in the rain beside the road? Don't do that on my account," he added, with a covetous look to where she was snapping out of her torpor and re-arranging her clothing.

Shell-shocked, she could only tuck, adjust and zip her jacket to her throat. "I didn't mean to let it go that far." How had it happened? What about her little speech about having found a spine against being pressured?

"I shouldn't have kissed you. I knew I wouldn't want to stop." He checked the mirrors, then fired the engine and pulled into the rain, the wipers slapping at full speed in the tiny windscreen. Reaching out to take her hand, he tangled his thick fingers between hers. The tiny stretch was sensual and erotic. He rested their clasped hands on the stick shift.

"It's okay. I have some in my room."

"Some—condoms?" So premeditated. If he'd pulled her to the wet grass a few seconds ago she would have gone without protest, but talking like this allowed reservations to creep in.

"Yes." The curt way he answered and the purposeful way he drove made it sound like they were on their way to pick up an organ transplant.

But his having condoms in his room made Rowan's hand go cold inside the vital grip of his. Did that mean he slept with women at Rosedale? All her insecurities flooded to the fore as she contemplated the scope of his sexual conquests. And she was signing up to be next? How demoralizing!

Twisting free of his grip, she swallowed back sick anxiety that grew all the more troubling when she realized he'd released her because he needed to shift down and make the turn into Rosedale. Seconds later they pulled into the garage. The absence of pounding rain made the interior of the car overly silent—especially once he cut the engine.

Feeling suffocated, Rowan threw herself out of the car, then stopped. She wanted to stomp away in a jealous temper because he'd confessed to having other women, but that would be immature. It wasn't as if she'd believed *he* was a virgin. Maybe it made her heart ache that he treated Rosedale like a brothel, but given the way its owner had caused him to feel left out in the cold could she really expect him to view the house as sacred and special the way she did?

Moodily shifting to the open garage door, she stared through the wall of water pouring off the eaves and hugged herself.

He'd had casual sex with a lot of women. Maybe sex with her would be equally casual for him, but it would mean something to her. Nic, her first, here at Rosedale.

Rowan pressed the backs of her knuckles against lips that began to quiver with vulnerability, edging toward one of the biggest decisions of her life.

"Ro?" Light fingers tickled over her hair, sending a shivery warmth cascading through her. His hand settled warmly on her shoulder.

Rowan turned her head to look up at him, catching her breath at the impact he made on her. He looked into her eyes and she saw a tiny flicker of something, almost a flinch, like he saw something in her gaze that struck past his impervious shell. His hand flexed and hot intent flowed back into his evening-blue eyes, burning out anything else she thought she might have seen.

"Will you come upstairs with me?"

She couldn't speak, but she nodded. His smile, warm and appreciative, softened his warrior features into something so handsome he stole her breath. He took her hand and led her into the house.

CHAPTER SIX

THIS was happening.

Nic's grip on her hand was warm and strong, holding her anchored when Rowan felt she might float away. This was one of those instances so perfect it was like a rainbow on a bubble—enchanting but fragile. She clung to his hand as they climbed the stairs, fearful something would break the spell and cause her tentative euphoria to burst.

When he led her to his door she hung back, trying not to reveal how much tension was gathering inside her.

His gaze searched hers and Rowan felt as though invisible threads looped out to cast around her and back to him, gathering them into a tight, inescapable cocoon. There was such smouldering sexuality in his face she feared for a moment that she was about to be overtaken by him, captured and smothered.

"Second thoughts?" he asked with gruff coolness.

Rowan looked down at the threshold she couldn't bring herself to cross. "Suffering a bit of performance anxiety. I don't want to disappoint you."

Nic surprised her by lifting her hand to press soft kisses on her cool fingers, his lips twitching with amusement. "You've come a long way. Twenty-four hours ago you didn't give a damn what I thought."

Rowan couldn't speak. The truth was too revealing.

She'd always cared. This was just the first time she was admitting it. The back of her throat stung. The moment was huge.

Nic's fingers tightened on hers. "You won't disappoint me," he said. "I've waited too long for this to be anything but completely gratifying." He leaned down and took her mouth in a slow kiss.

She clung to his lips with her own, prolonging the exquisite rightness, letting the soft kiss play out into intensifying rhythms that made her hurt inside. It was so good.

Nic was barely hanging on to a rational thought. Rowan's mouth was petal-soft and she smelled like a warm summer garden: earthy and rosy and fresh. He could feel little tremors striking deep within her as he kissed her. That delicious quiver fed the answering energy prickling under his skin as the taste of her nape was imprinted against his open lips. When she lifted her arms around his neck and pressed closer, delicately clashing into his achingly aroused flesh, his mind exploded.

He tightened his hold on her, reveling in the restless, inciting quest of her mouth. With a groan, he picked her up, never having done anything so feverish in his life. She leapt into a firm bundle against his chest, like she'd done it a thousand times—which he dimly supposed she had, on the stage and possibly for other men.

He ducked the thought, concentrating on how she was light and slender and so much more earnest than he'd expected. *Performer*, he reminded himself, but he responded to her passion all the same, fully involved in their kiss as he carried her into the room.

He should have kept this on neutral territory, he thought dimly, but assured himself that Rowan wouldn't have unrealistic expectations. She'd been around the block.

Setting her on her feet, he pressed her away long enough

to open her jacket. They were both breathing hard, and she shrugged out of the short coat to let it fall to the floor with an impatience he applauded. He wished he could muster a smile of satisfaction, but desire was throbbing in him like an imperative. He threw his own shirt off and kicked away his shoes.

Rowan grasped his arm and bent one leg to unzip her long boot. The second one was released and she stepped out of them, so much shorter than she seemed when her larger than life personality was on full display. This Rowan was…

Vulnerable.

For all her urgency there was a shyness in the way she hesitated with her hands on the snap of her jeans, her pillowy bottom lip caught between her teeth. "Should we… um…close the door?"

Her modesty took him aback, turning over places in him he'd buried under years of jaded enjoyment of women without engaging with them. He had a distant thought to drawl a somewhat tasteless, *Who's going to come in*? but found a shred of a gentlemanly behavior instead. He turned to press the door closed.

And as the click echoed in the silent room the word *gentleman* mocked him. *"What are your intentions, Nic? Men like you…"*

Nic curled a fist against the seam of the closed door, fighting the invasion of the dark memory. He and Rowan had cleared the air. He believed her. They wanted each other; it was as simple as that. This had nothing to do with intentions and futures. It was two adults coming together in mutual desire. Not the sort of thing Olief should have had any disdain for, given the way he'd fathered a child from one mistress and lived in sin for nearly a decade with another.

Rowan had fumbled her jeans open, but couldn't bring

herself to peel them down while Nic had his back to her. Having him watch her wouldn't make it easier, but her self-confidence was draining fast as he leaned on the door like that, tension gathering across his naked shoulders. He had such a beautiful back, strong and tanned, powerful muscles shifting as though he was bearing up under a great weight.

"Nic? Are you—?" *Having second thoughts?* She would *die*.

He brought his head up and turned. Desire flared past whatever dark thoughts had taken him for a split second. His avid glance made her feel beautiful even though she wasn't any kind of sex goddess. Her hair was wind-whipped, she wore next to no makeup, and was probably pale with the stagefright that was threatening on the periphery. But he strode forward with purpose and cupped her head, kissing her like he had in the car—like he would spontaneously combust if he didn't do it this second.

It was the reassurance she needed. Grasping his head, she kissed him back with all the passion in her, grateful and excited and swimming in rising desire. When he began to peel up her top she lifted her arms to help him. It landed in a purple stain in the middle of the floor and was quickly topped by her bra.

Nic dragged her close, and the contact of his hard, hair-roughened chest on her breasts undid her. She melted, fingers splaying wide to touch as much of him as possible, while she slowly writhed against his sensuous heat and turned her lips into his throat.

He said her name and swore, then said raggedly, "I'm trying to find a little finesse here, but—" His fingertips swept her spine and shoulderblades before he brought his hands forward and sweetly captured her breasts.

"It's okay. I'm in a hurry too..."

He groaned and his hands gently crushed her curves as

he crowded into her, covering her mouth once, hard, before he stepped back and pulled off his jeans. He skimmed his shorts off with them and knocked the crumpled heap away with his foot, straightening before her with feet braced.

A purely female ache of longing clenched deep inside her as she took in his wide chest and taut flat stomach, powerful thighs and even more powerfully thick erection. She swallowed as she measured him with her eyes, intimidated.

Nic opened hands that had curled into tense fists and stepped close to begin easing her jeans down her hips. He loomed tall and potent, his penis brushing her stomach as his mouth touched her shoulder.

Rowan made herself breathe, but it was shaky, and she wasn't getting nearly enough oxygen. As he lowered the clinging denim down her thighs she trembled, wriggling to help him and stepping out of them quickly so she could rush back against him, hiding, but deeply affected. She had never been naked with a man, never touched one like this, and she desperately wanted to give Nic pleasure.

Pressing for a little space, she clasped him lightly and gasped, shocked by how silky he felt. Satin over steel. He seemed to thicken and harden in her tentative hold and his big hand covered hers once, the single stroke a too brief lesson before he peeled her hand away and brought her palm to his mouth.

"I don't want to disappoint you either," he said wryly, and edged her backward, effortlessly levering her onto the bed beneath him.

Rowan couldn't find her voice, too besieged by each tiny sensation she was trying to memorize. Nic's weight beside her on the mattress. His hand massaging her belly as he kissed her again. His tongue stroking over hers so it felt like hot honey gathered between her thighs. His heavy thigh rested across hers, holding still the legs that wanted to pedal in sensual pleasure. The burning rod of his penis was rampant against her hip. She couldn't touch enough of him, couldn't process all the delicious parts of him when her blood pressure was rising in relentless increments.

He slid down a little, his tongue going to her nipple, his knee pressing between her thighs to part her legs. He very lightly stroked the crease where her thighs met plump folds. She grew acutely sensitive under his barely there fondling, her tangled nerve-endings gathering in a storm of greedy hunger. She tried to turn into him, wanting more contact, but he took her nipple deep in his mouth and parted her with knowledgeable fingers.

Pleasure struck like a hammer-blow, making her groan unabashedly. He deepened his caress, stroking and circling, gently invading, then teasing again, repeating the play so the meltdown became a build-up.

"Nic," she moaned, dragging at his hair to lift his head.

He looked at her like he was drugged and swept a hand out. Efficient and quick, he protected them both, then shifted to cover her.

She experienced a stab of nervousness again. Her legs twitched as they parted on either side of his hips. She bent her knees, instinctively wanting to embrace him with her thighs. Every part of her wanted to gather him in. He was so strong and fiercely beautiful with that intense expression on his face, looking down at her like she was the most incredible thing he'd ever seen. Her nipples were shards of crystal that wanted to pierce into him as his chest came down on hers, heavy and firm.

And then he pressed into her.

Rowan caught her breath, startled by the shocking intimacy of the act. It hurt a little, but she was so aroused she didn't care. She ached for the stimulation of pressure and stretching as she felt the thickness of him invade.

"Rowan," he said raggedly, his expression a little bewildered beneath his flush of extreme arousal, "you're—"

"Don't be mad, Nic," she urged, curling her legs around him in a vice-like trap, using her lean strength to pull him in and impale herself a little more. She couldn't help the gasping cry that left her. It felt so extraordinary. "I want this. I want it to be you."

"—so tight," he ground through clenched teeth, demonstrating how strong he was by keeping her from forcing the penetration. He shuddered and gave her an incredulous look. "You *liar*," he breathed, then kissed her possessively while he very, very slowly and oh, so carefully let the weight of his hips settle on her.

And gently, inexorably, his flesh drove all the way into hers.

Rowan tipped back her head and moaned in exultation.

She belonged to him. Now and forever.

Nic kissed her again and again—long, languorous kisses on her lips and sweet caresses down her throat and across her shoulders. Rowan melted under his attention, not realizing how much tension her muscles had gathered until it eased away.

That was when he groaned and started to withdraw, making her protest and cling to him in ways she hadn't realized she could. He came back, body trembling with the effort to discipline himself. It was a control she instantly felt compelled to shatter.

Rowan stroked her hands over his arms and shoulders, lightly raking her nails down to his buttocks. Nic's hips jerked into hers. It hurt, but the friction, the fullness, was so good at the same time. The conflict of wanting to self-protect and yet let him push her toward the pinnacle made her scrape her nails down his back again. He caught her wrists and flattened her hands beneath his, sealing their palms together. With a glitter of pure animal need in his flame-blue eyes he increased the pace, becoming relentless and remorseless, feeding her tension until everything in her began to gather.

It was astonishing. She couldn't hold on, couldn't hold back. "Nic!" She squeezed her legs around him, suddenly feeling the heart-stopping culmination very close. She didn't want it to end! She fought giving in, but wanted it so badly. He kept thrusting and her body clenched on his shaft, as if she could hold him forever. He drew her nerve-endings to their very limit…

And then…

Release.

Everything dimmed for a heartbeat before the cataclysm struck deep within her. Shattering pleasure was carried outward in waves of abject joy. Rowan could only receive him, feeling the writhe of his hard muscles as he released a guttural shout and drove deep. The pulses of his tremendous climax were visceral, playing against her own so they were locked in an exquisite paroxysm. She'd never felt so close to anyone in her life. His name pulsed in her head with the crashing throb of their mutual release. *Nic, Nic, Nic.*

The final sob of ecstasy was hers. For the end that was so beautiful and so unbearable. She wanted to stay joined with him forever, but a final shudder jolted through him and her own climactic pulses began to fade. Still breathing hard, he carefully disengaged and rolled away.

The wordless removal of physical contact smacked her with the savage brutality of casual sex. She'd felt on the edge of a burgeoning beauty, something so profound it filled her chest and made her eyes dampen with happiness. Having him pull away left her instantly bereft. His back was to her and his feet were bound to hit the floor any second. The door would be next.

Appalled to find herself near tears, Rowan swallowed a pained cry and rolled to her side of the bed, starting to swing her feet off. She could make it to the bathroom before he walked out. It would save a shred of her dignity to not be the one left in the bed.

A thick arm snaked around her and a heavy leg scooped hers back to the middle of the mattress. He was so *hot*. She instinctively pushed her hands against his damp chest where his heartbeat still raced. He carried her hands to a point above her head, trapping them in his own while his massive body engulfed hers in a blanket of hard muscle.

"Wait," he growled, breath still short. "*Why me*, Rowan?"

CHAPTER SEVEN

Nic felt as though he was looking at a stranger—one so beautiful she made his heart lurch. Her eyelids were swollen under a smoky smudge of makeup, her green irises like rain-soaked moss, her lips ripened by his kisses. He pulled back a little for a lengthy study of every flushed curve and trembling muscle.

How in the hell was he the only man who'd ever seen her like this?

Rowan wriggled in muted protest. He was still aroused enough for rational thought to recede and instinct to want to take over. She was so smooth and soft, her warmed scent a soporific drug to his senses. The desire to sink down on her and rediscover every decadent inch of her increased.

His heartbeat elevated, but she stiffened in wariness.

"What are you doing?"

She sounded breathless. Her flat stomach contracted under the weight of his hand while her wrists turned in the light grip of his other hand. Her flexing was a seductive trigger he fought out of self-preservation. This situation didn't make sense and he needed it to.

"I'm admiring this gift you've given me." Her springy curls begged for petting, but he resisted, taking heed of her belligerently angled chin instead.

"You don't have to be so sarcastic about it," she said.

"I'm not trying to be sarcastic. I'm stunned." Winded. Very much in danger of being *moved*. He had to stick to cool analysis or he'd begin attaching meaning to this unique circumstance. He had worried being in his bedroom would make the act too personal, but she had shot things into a realm of intimate sharing that didn't happen often between any two people—most especially between him and anyone.

"How, Ro? There was a boy at school. I heard the stories."

Her lips firmed and her cheeks darkened. "That...didn't work out. I thought I was ready, but I wasn't. I called it off. He was getting dressed when the headmistress found us. Would you let go of me, please?"

He released her and she sat up. Her narrow back seemed very vulnerable. He felt an unaccountable urge to pull her back into his embrace and keep her sheltered against him. A curious lump formed in his chest. She'd been so tight. Exquisite and succulent. Her rippling orgasm had been unmistakable, but her sheath new and small. If he'd hurt her he'd never forgive himself.

"Are you all right?"

"Fine. You?" Rowan flipped the edge of the coverlet up and across her front, dying with self-consciousness. "Shall we have a post-mortem on *your* past, too? Did you get it right the first time, or do you have an inept experience you'd like to share?"

Nic was impervious to the glare she sent over her shoulder. He sprawled as comfortably as any male animal whose appetite had been recently sated. The condom was gone, she noted—with a glance that he caught.

His brows went up while his eyelids stayed heavy.

She prickled with embarrassment, willing to give anything to take back that peek. He was still hard. Had he not been satisfied? The coverlet bunched thickly in her hands as she curled her fingers into apprehensive fists.

"I'm not trying to pry," he said. "I just can't understand how you'd still be a virgin when I've seen you with men I thought were your lovers."

"Who? Dance partners? We're all very familiar. It doesn't mean anything." Kind of like how this act seemed to have no profundity for him beyond a mystery to be solved.

She couldn't believe she had felt apprehensive at the thought of him walking out. This was far worse—sitting naked next to him, insanely aware of what they'd just done, how he'd touched her like he not only owned her but knew her body's responses better than she did, trying to have a conversation.

Her entire world had been flooded with color. A huge bubble of elation had threatened to split her chest. But he didn't need time to savor and process. He wasn't suffering any craving for reassurance. He'd done this a thousand times.

A thousand and one.

"You might have offered a clue," he chided dryly.

"Like what? Can you imagine Cassandra O'Brien's daughter running around wearing one of those 'Proud To Be A Virgin' bracelets? I was happy people thought I'd been with that boy. My school friends quit teasing me. I dated when I could, but my schedule didn't allow for anything long-term so sex never happened."

"I meant you might have said something today." His voice changed, becoming darker and crisper.

She sensed that word *long-term* had done it and swallowed. He didn't move, but she watched a new level of coolness come over him. It made the tiny inch of space between them seem cavernous and the warm room grow cold.

"Why would you throw it away on me?" he asked.

Throw it away. Her stomach clenched. Not exactly a treasured moment. More like taking out the garbage. She hated herself then for not being able to control who she was attracted to. For letting that attraction rule her to the point of waiting half her life for him and then giving herself despite knowing it meant nothing to him.

Yet when she tried to conjure regret all she felt was a stunned ache of poignant joy. It had been the most singularly beautiful experience of her life. She was glad it had been with Nic.

"Do you really think virginity is something precious to be bottled up and hoarded for a special occasion?" she asked with a catch in her voice, trying to hide how deeply stirred she was as she reached back to brace herself on her arm and face him. Her other hand held the coverlet firmly across her breasts and thighs, but she did her best to mirror his nonchalance, affecting only vague interest.

His gaze cut a swift glance at her nude shoulders and exposed knee before meeting hers again. "I guess I wouldn't be a very progressive man if I did, but I imagine you've had other opportunities, so choosing to give it up now—with me—seems odd."

"Why not you?" she challenged, her heart dancing close to a tricky ledge.

His intense look of concentration blanked for a second into a hollow gaze before he shuttered his expression. "Indeed, why not me when any man would do? Why *now* is the real question, isn't it?"

An urge to correct him caught in her throat, but she didn't want to reveal how much she had wanted it to be him. At the same time a stunning insight struck her. Nic had no idea he was special to her or anyone else. She had been told all her life that she was special—so special she had to live up to unrealistic expectations—but he hadn't had that problem. His father had ignored him. What about his mother?

Rowan ached to ask, but prying was out of place. He wouldn't appreciate it, given what a proud, aloof man he was. She let her hair fall forward to hide her frown of empathetic pain.

"I was tired of fighting with you. Fighting that feeling," she confessed, hoping he wouldn't make her tell him exactly how long that feeling had been twisting like a flame inside her. Tossing her hair back, she made a false attempt at flippancy. "And you're the one who thinks I need to grow up, so it's rather fitting for you to be the one to make me a woman, don't you think?"

A disturbing sense of privilege poured into Nic. Plainly this act held a lot less importance to her than it did for him, so he did his best to laugh it off the way she had. "Is that what this was? A coming-of-age ceremony?"

For a second he thought Rowan flinched. A familiar bleak valley threatened to swallow up his brief sense of pride. He tensed, but then Rowan produced a wide smile that was like light breaking over the dark edges that surrounded him, bathing him in reprieve. She cupped the side of his face, leaning close enough to touch a light kiss to his mouth.

"Yes, Nic. You might not be given to sentimentality about these things, but I shall forever look back on you fondly as My First. That's almost as good as whatever you get for being Newsman of the Year, isn't it?"

Always so glib, but her words had a profound effect on him. That *forever look back* ought to be reassuring. He had barely let himself acknowledge the fear that her taking him as her first lover and dropping words like *long-term* meant she expected a relationship. He most certainly was not the man to give her anything like that.

But that *fondly* squeezed feeling out of his incompetent heart. Two days ago he wouldn't have given any thought to parting with animosity between them, but quite suddenly he hoped for something better than that.

She started to pull away and he brought his hand to the back of her head, silky curls crushed under his gentle insistence she stay close.

"I won't forget this either," he admitted.

Which scared him as much as the vulnerable way Rowan caught her lip between her teeth. He closed his eyes against a look that searched for reassurance and drew her forward so he could kiss her, making her release her bottom lip to his own gentle bite and lingering attention to soothe any tenderness he inflicted.

The kiss quickly got out of hand and he groaned, never having come up against anything like this: the desire to make love again so soon after the most intense orgasm of his life, or with a woman so new to it she couldn't.

When she breathed his name against his lips and set a hand on his collarbone he had to let her put space between them.

"Are you saying you won't forget in a good way or a bad way?"

Was she kidding? He glanced down at the raging muscle straining from between his thighs like a compass needle seeking North.

"I know. I'm sorry." Her flush was pure mortification. "I thought it was good for both of us, but—"

"Maybe if you're willing to practice we can do something about it?" he chided facetiously.

Rowan paled and he realized with horror that she'd taken it the wrong way. She tried to bolt from the bed and again he had to grab her, holding tight to her wiry strength while she struggled and slapped at him.

"That was a joke," he insisted, trying to speak over her angry demands to quit manhandling her. He wouldn't let her go, though—not when his heart was bottoming out at how badly he'd misread her sensitivity. "Rowan, listen. *Ouch*." He swore as he took a scratch down his rib cage before he immobilized her.

"That wasn't funny, Nic!" She was breathing hard, muscles a taut bundle of resistance against his hold, eyes spitting venom. "I know more about practice than anyone, and I'll be damned if I'm going back to trying and not getting it right. For *you*. I'm living for me now—understand? I don't care if it was good for you. It was good for me, so you can go to hell with your *practice*."

His chest knotted up so tight he could barely breathe.

"It *was* good for me," he insisted, pressing the words into her temple as she turned a stubborn cheek against him. He could see her brow pleated in hurt.

He didn't know how to apologize with the kind of sincerity needed here, and inadequacy threatened to push him out of the room rather than try, but he had learned enough about her in the last two days to realize how deeply it would injure her to think her performance had failed to please him.

"I only meant I want to make love again and I realize you won't want to." He hurried to say it, shifting because he was aroused by their tussle and unable to hide it. He didn't expect anything but a cold shower, though. "You have this insane effect on me, Ro. You always have. I can't help it."

She turned her head to look at him and he began to wobble on a tightrope a thousand stories in the air. He backed onto solid ground.

"I don't know what it is with our chemistry. I had hoped

once would be enough." The lie bunched his muscles into aching knots. He had *never* believed once would be enough. "If you let me, I'd be on you night and day to work this out of my system."

Her lashes came down to hide her eyes and he scowled, uncomfortable with how much he'd revealed. He was generally self-sufficient, but now he looked into a bleak future where his frustrating hunger for her might actually be worse, not easier to bear.

"If we were coming together as equals," she said carefully, before she lifted wary lashes, "I'd let you. But not if I don't have the sort of experience to keep you interested."

"You—" she couldn't see the fine tremble in the hand he used to smooth her hair "—are a natural. I'm at the disadvantage. I know how special this is."

"Tell all the girls that, do you?"

"I've never said it to anyone," he contradicted tightly.

"Really?" She rolled into him with a forgiving slither of silken skin and inviting softness, bending his mind away from the alarm bells against making comparisons or revealing how truly exceptional their experience was.

Her pleased smile provoked another zing of warning against feeding her ego and that sense of entitlement to adoration of hers. He didn't want to be a slave to her good graces. But her light hands skimmed over him in deliciously arousing paths, rewarding rather than rejecting, and he quit caring that he was turning into one more ardent fan.

"Me, too. Best ever." She strained to touch her lips under his chin.

With a shaken chuckle and deep reluctance he stopped her. This mood of hers was surprisingly endearing. Gathering her slender fingers in his own, he kissed the scrape on her palm before saying, "You need time to recover. Don't you?"

"No. I like the way you make me feel, Nic. I want to do it again."

The tiny throb of longing in her voice was a golden rope that looped around the root of him and tugged.

He shuddered and gave in, tucking her under him with possessive intent.

One thing about Rosedale, Nic acknowledged later that evening, if you wanted to avoid someone you could.

He'd left her as the sky was starting to darken. Rowan had been on her stomach, nothing but a midnight waterfall of hair and an ivory shoulder. His body had sprung to attention despite the way he'd worked it into exhaustion over hours of lovemaking. He'd forced himself to leave her, partly because he was sure she was tender and partly because he hated how addicted he was becoming.

Becoming? a voice taunted deep in his head. He'd always been obsessed. Now he'd had her it was worse. And he'd *admitted* it to her. That left him deeply uneasy, so he had showered, dressed, come into his office and shut the door.

The memory of Rowan's uninhibited response wasn't as easy to leave behind. At one point she'd kissed her way down his body and murmured, "May I? I've always wondered..." He'd disbelieved she was *that* inexperienced, but the amateur way she'd learned to please him had told him this too was her first time and had nearly undone him.

He glanced at his knuckles, going white where he gripped the arm of his chair. He ought to be working, not reliving Rowan's teasing him beyond bearing before lifting to ride his hips until she was sobbing with rapture.

His laptop hummed with yet another string of emails hitting his inbox, but he wasn't having much luck being productive and he needed to be. The conglomerate of multimedia interests that Olief had amassed during his lifetime was a demanding operation. If Nic hadn't had this to consume him for the last year, the fruitless search for Olief's plane and its survivors might have driven him to madness.

Lately he'd taken more of his own direction, but he couldn't do it properly until Olief was declared dead and the will was read. Uncertainty hovered around him like the buzz of a mosquito as he considered what it might reveal. He *liked* running things. He wanted to continue to do so. And if it turned out Olief had not named him as his heir…

Nic turned away from the thought, telling himself to be prepared for anything—even that. But it would sting. In the meantime he drew a salary as the interim president by keeping the place running and solvent. He ought to be doing that, not frittering away his time between brooding over things he couldn't change and schoolboy fantasies about Rowan's breasts filling his hands.

Hunger of every kind gripped him. The kind that made him reach to adjust himself in the confines of his jeans and the kind that growled in his empty stomach.

A thought flitted through his mind of taking Rowan down to the ferry landing for a meal. But they weren't dating. He didn't know what they were doing, he acknowledged with a hard scrape of his hand down his face.

Impatient, he flung open the door and was greeted by the surprising scent of… Whatever it was, it smelled delicious. He followed it downstairs.

Rowan hadn't expected her return to Rosedale to be like this. When she'd made the decision to come she'd imagined having the house to herself, perhaps sharing a few light meals with Anna, but mostly taking stock of her life and figuring out her next steps.

She was doing a little of that—or perhaps it was more accurate to say she was absorbing the fact that she was going to have to do some really hard thinking on that front since Nic had cut off her income. Her mind didn't want to pin itself to those sorts of thoughts, though. It was too busy trying to make sense of the passionate affair she'd started with the one man she'd always believed out of reach. She had never imagined this could really happen. Nevertheless, she and Nic had spent hours reading each other like braille text, with his masculine groans of passion filling the air as often as her cries of delight.

Excitement flushed through her as she recalled drawing those sounds from him. At the same time she had to keep reminding herself it was a temporary arrangement. Perhaps he'd given her orgasms at an exponential rate to his own, maybe he'd even admitted that she had *always* had an effect on him, but he'd been the first to leave. She bit her lip, preferring the pain of her teeth over the insecure ache his leaving had caused. Waking with him would have been reassuring. Sweet, even.

"What are you making?"

She squeaked in startlement and almost dropped the whole spice jar into the pot. One glance over her shoulder flashed a million sensual memories through her mind. Her palms began to sweat and she could barely hold the wooden spoon to stir the sauce when she turned back to the stove. Hopefully he'd blame the steam off the pan for the dampness around her hairline.

"Braised beef and roasted vegetables," she answered.

He came to peer over her shoulder, hands settling on her waist. His nearness made her fingers even more nerveless. "Ambitious. Spaghetti would have been fine."

"Oh, you know what they say about the way to a man's heart."

His hands dropped from her waist and she felt a frigid blast move into the space he'd occupied as he moved away.

She made herself laugh, because the alternative was to let his reaction pierce her to the bone. "Apparently we both need to work on taking a joke." She stepped away to reach for her ice water with lemon, using it to ease the constriction in her throat. "The truth is I know my way around a kitchen quite well. One of Mum's nearest and dearests was a French chef. He taught me to put on an evening that allowed Mum to portray the lifestyle to which she aspired." Rowan licked that delicate wording off her cold lips. "So I have one more useless skill in my bag of tricks. I brought in that Bordeaux, if you want a glass." She nodded at the bottle.

"Why is it useless?" He found the bottle opener and cut the wax off the cork.

"Because I don't like cooking to order, and I'm not certified."

He pondered that as he poured a glass and brought out a second one.

"No, thanks," she said to forestall him.

"You don't want any?"

"There's a difference between wanting and needing. I would like a glass. I'm sure it's very nice—look at the year—but I'd rather refuse and prove I don't need it."

"You really did a number on yourself after leaving school, didn't you?"

"You haven't said anything I haven't said to myself," she assured him with a wan smile, recollecting the morning she'd woken with gaps in her memory and a reflection that reminded her too much of her father. It had been a bit of a relief to find her virginity intact, actually.

Turning away from his penetrating look, she removed a tray of hors d'oeuvres from the refrigerator. "To tide you over?" she invited.

He offered a whistle of appreciation at the array of tiny

pastries, some topped with caviar and hot relish, all arranged between bites of cheese and colorful olives. Rowan quietly glowed under his approval, pleased she could wow him in this way at least.

"You've never had a problem with alcohol, have you?" She realized she'd never seen him drunk and that it was probably one of the things that attracted her most about him. He epitomized the self-possessed social drinker. "Even with all those horrible things you saw as a correspondent?"

"I don't like inhibiting my ability to control myself or any given situation."

"Oh, there's a surprise!" she said on a bubble of mirth. "You must have given your mother a lot of grief with that attitude." She stole his glass of wine long enough to tilt a splash into the sauce before she stirred it and began plating their meals.

His silence brought her head up.

"I'm sorry—is your mother alive?" she asked with a skip of compunction. "I didn't mean—"

"It's fine," he dismissed. "Yes, she is. And I don't believe I was a problem for her until her husband realized I wasn't his. That's when I was sent to boarding school. I didn't see her after that."

Rowan felt a little shock go through her. Her ears grasped for more, but he didn't expound. With a little frown she concentrated on quickly fanning slices of beef like a tiny hand of cards on the plates. After arranging the vegetables in a colorful crescent around golden potato croquettes, she zig-zagged sauce across the meat, added an asparagus spear decoratively wrapped with prosciutto, dabbed mustard sauce and tiny slivers of cucumber onto it, then a final garnish of a few sprigs of watercress and a radish flower.

"The dining room is set. Can you get the door?"

He followed and held her chair before seating himself and giving his plate the admiration it deserved. "This looks as good as it smells."

"Tuck in." His appreciation suffused her in warmth, but she couldn't shake the chill from what he'd revealed. As he picked up his cutlery, she ventured, "Nic, I can't help asking… Are you saying your mother never came to see you at school?"

CHAPTER EIGHT

THE beef melted on his tongue, prepared better than anything any chef he'd ever hired had managed. Nevertheless, it still might have been a slice of his own heart filetted onto the plate, given the way it stuck to the roof of his mouth.

He should have kept his mouth shut. His entire life had been shattered when the truth of his parentage had come to light. It was not something he talked about, and yet it had flowed out uncontrolled with only a sip of red wine to lubricate it. Because he was relaxed by sex? Because physical closeness had fooled him into feeling emotionally comfortable with Rowan?

What to do now? If he refused to speak of it she'd know it was something that still had the power to wring out his insides.

At the same time there was an angry part of him that wanted to take her view of Olief and shake it up, make her see he wasn't a superhero. He was flawed. Or Nic was. He'd never figured that one out—whether it was his parents' deficiency or his own.

"Who was she? I mean, how did Olief know her?"

Her curiosity was not the lurid kind. He might have stood that. No, her brow wore a wrinkle of concern. She had never been ignored, so she didn't understand how any child could be.

Again the deep fear that *he* was the problem pealed inside him.

"He didn't know her. Not really," he said, keeping his tone neutral. "She was an airline hostess. He said it happened as he was coming back from being away in some ugly place."

"Do you think he did that often? Mum was always terrified he'd cheat on her because he'd cheated on his first wife, but— Wait. Don't tell me." Rowan held up a hand, face turning away. "It would kill me to hear that he did."

"I have no idea," Nic said flatly. "He didn't have any other children. I'm quite sure of that. That was the reason he didn't want his wife knowing about me. They tried their entire marriage to have a baby and she couldn't conceive."

The briefest flinch of anguish spasmed across her features, too quick for him to be sure he'd seen it before it dissolved in a frown of incomprehension. "But if he wanted children why didn't he see *you*?"

"He was ashamed of me."

Her eyes widened and her jaw slackened, but she quickly recovered, shaking her head. "You don't know that."

"He told me, Rowan. I asked him that exact question and that's what he said."

"He was ashamed of *himself.* If not, he should have been," she said, with a quick flare of vehement temper.

Her anger, when Olief was like a god to her, surprised him, cracking into and touching an internal place he kept well protected. His breath backed up in his lungs.

"Why didn't your mother do something? Insist he acknowledge you. Or did she? You said he paid for your education?" Rowan pressed.

"He paid for my schooling, yes." Nic set two fingertips on the bottom of his wineglass, lining it up with precision against the subtle pattern in the tablecloth. Every word he released seemed to scald all the way up his esophagus. "She didn't make a fuss because I was her shameful secret, too. She hadn't told her husband that she was already pregnant when they married. When he found out she took what Olief was willing to give her—tuition at a boarding school so they could all pretend I didn't exist."

Rowan had a small appetite at the best of times, but it evaporated completely as she took in the chilling rejection Nic had suffered. He was very much contained within his aloof shell at the moment, his muscles a tense barrier that accentuated what a tough, strong man he'd become, but shades of baffled shame still lingered in his eyes.

Everything in her ached with the longing to rise and wrap her arms around him, to try and repair the damage done, but she was learning. This was why he was always on his guard. He'd been hurt—terribly. Rowan had no trouble believing Olief had wanted to shield his wife, but to hurt a child? His own son?

"How...?" She took a sip of water to clear her thickened throat. "How did the truth come out?" she asked numbly.

Nic pointed at his hair. "My mother and her husband are both Greek, both dark. Babies and toddlers might sometimes have blond hair, but by the time I was entering school and still a towhead, not to mention looking nothing like the man I thought of as my father, it was obvious a goose egg had been hatched with the ducks."

Rowan dropped her cutlery, unable to fully comprehend what he was saying. "So he supported sending you away? After years of believing he was your father? What sort of relationship do you have with him now?"

"None. Once my mother admitted I wasn't his he never spoke to me again." Nic spoke without inflection, his delivery like a newscast.

"You can't be serious."

"He was a bastard. It was no loss to me." He applied himself to his meal.

Rowan cast for something solid to grasp on to as a painful sea of confusion swirled around her. "You can't tell me that everyone who was supposed to be acting like a parent in your life just stuck you in some horrible boarding school like you were a criminal to be sent to prison."

With eyes half-closed in a laconic, flinty stare, he took a deep swallow of wine. "I didn't mind boarding school. I had the brains and the brawn that allowed a person to succeed there, and I realized quickly that I was on my own so I'd better seize the opportunity. What's in this sauce besides wine? It's very good."

Rowan soaked in the tub, still reeling under the blows Nic had been dealt as a child. He'd barely said another word after his stunning revelations, only cleaned his plate and excused himself to work.

Rowan had almost let out a hysterical laugh as he'd walked away. She so recognized that remote, unreachable man. All those years when she'd heard him described as Olief's estranged son she'd blamed Nic. Nic was the one who showed up at Olief's invitation like he was doing Olief a favor. Nic was the one who never left so much as a spare toothbrush in the rooms set aside for him. Nic was the one who took off for hours in his black roadster, never saying where he was going or when he'd be back.

Olief had so much to answer for.

Rowan was angry with him. Furious. He'd broken something in Nic. The boy had needed his real father to step up when his supposed one had rejected him. Instead Olief's disregard had made Nic incapable of trusting in human relationships. How could Olief have done it? Why?

With a pang, she faced that she'd never know—although

she wouldn't be surprised if it had something to do with the harsh mental toll Nic had mentioned with regard to being a foreign correspondent. Olief had been doing that sort of work then. Perhaps Olief simply hadn't had anything to offer his son.

It still made Rowan ache to reach out to Nic and heal him in some way—not that she imagined he'd let her. If anything, he probably resented letting her draw so much out of him. That was why he'd locked himself in his office again.

Drying herself off, she brushed out her hair and wondered if she should go to him, not sure she could face being rebuffed if he shut her out.

With a yawn, she counted the hours of sleep she'd got last night—not many, as she'd tried to work out ways to talk Nic around to her views on Rosedale. She'd slept after their vigorous hours in bed, but not for long. Once she'd woken to find him gone she'd risen and started work in the kitchen. Now her soak in the tub had filled her with lethargy.

She set her head on her pillow for a moment and picked up her feet. She was a master at catnaps....

Nic nudged open the bedroom door and took in Sleeping Beauty, one hand tucked beneath her folded knees, the other curled under her chin like a child. Her hair was a tumbled mass, her lips a red bow, her face free of makeup and her breath soft. She was as innocent as they made them.

While *he'd* finally given in to the guilty tension swirling like a murky cloud through him and come searching for release. Base, masculine, primordial forgetfulness. His flesh responded to the nearness of hers with a predictable rush of readiness, blood flooding into his crotch so fast it hurt.

Her being asleep was a gift, he acknowledged with sour

irony. He hated being so weak as to be unable to resist her. If her eyes opened and flashed at him he'd be lost. If she woke and rolled onto her back—

He bit back a groan and reached for the coverlet, folding it from the far side of the bed until it wafted gently over her. This was better. She was getting too far under his skin with her fancy meals and empathetic speeches. This was supposed to be about sex. That was how he'd rationalized it and it was the only way they could come together.

Rowan's shock this evening perturbed him. She had ideals about family that were completely at odds with his own experience. It worried him, made him think that at some point she'd look to him to reflect some of those values and he simply didn't have them.

Uncurling his tense fists, he moved stiffly to the door, reminding himself that he might want to relieve sexual frustration with Rowan, but he didn't *need* to. He didn't need *her*.

He was on the beach, cold waves lapping at his knees, before he could draw a breath and begin to think clearly again.

Rowan's confusion at waking with the coverlet dragged across her was too sensitive a topic to pick apart first thing in the morning—especially when a nameless agitation made her feel so aware, like her skin had been stroked by a velvet breeze all evening and then it had been too hot to sleep.

Yet it was another windy day of scudding clouds and intermittent rain.

Nic was locked in his office down the hall, not looking for her. Or rather he had come looking and then left without touching her, leaving her heart as skinned as her knee, tight and tender and itchy. Which was juvenile.

The only way to suffocate her sense of irrelevance was to face up to another heartache of equal anguish. She went into the master bedroom and spent a long time with a sleeve held to her cheek, a collar to her nose, whole gowns clutched to her chest.

"You're a little old for dress-up, aren't you?" Nic's voice, rich and cool as ice cream, broke the silence an hour later, prompting a shiver of guilt and pleasure.

Rowan's first instinct was to toss aside the scarf she was tying over her hair and throw herself at him. She made herself finish knotting it in the famed Cassandra O'Brien style, then faced him. "People always tell me I look like Mum and I say thank you. But is it a compliment?"

"She was very beautiful, and so are you—but not because you resemble her."

Rowan blushed, but more because the admiration in his gaze was unabashedly sexual. She swallowed back the silly excited lump rising in her throat, trying to hold her wobbly smile steady as she loosened the scarf.

"What did you come in here for, full of such extravagant compliments? Keep that up and you'll see how much I resemble her when it comes to…" she tilted him her mother's infamous man-eater smile "…encouraging male admiration."

Something fierce and dangerous flashed in his Nordic blue eyes before he strolled forward on predatory feet. "I'm quite aware of how much you encourage it. I've seen you lay on the charm time and again. Why? Are you really as insecure as she was?"

His disparagement didn't allow her for one minute to think his attitude stemmed from jealousy or possessiveness.

Yanking the scarf off her neck with a burn of her nape and a cloud of painfully familiar sandalwood, Rowan replaced it on the hook beside the mirror. "How am I supposed to know what I am when I've always been told who to speak to, where to go and how to act?"

She moved away from him, angry and hurt that he was judging her and, yes, insecure. How could she develop an identity if her ability to make decisions had so rarely been tested?

"When Mum sent me to Paris I thought I'd finally be able to make more of my own choices, but it didn't work out that way. That was partly my fault, of course. The more I put into dance, the more I wanted to succeed to prove to myself I could. It's not easy to walk away from that much investment. It's like gambling. I kept thinking the next production would be the one that put me on the front of the stage, not the back. Mum would finally be happy and I'd be free to strike out *then*." She hitched her shoulder, lashed by how nascent and unrealistic that dream had been.

"And when you finally did have the chance you drank your face off and scared yourself," he said, from where he'd stayed behind her.

"I did," she agreed with a chuckle of defeated acknowledgment, elbows sharp in her palms and shoulder blades aching with tension. "The grief and guilt didn't help with that." She sighed, still ashamed of the way she'd behaved, but she had to move past it. She was determined to.

She pivoted to offer him a laissez-faire smile.

"So now I'm back at ground zero—the only place where I sometimes had moments of feeling like I knew who I was and what I wanted. I'm hoping for inspiration, but it eludes me. You're a worldly man. Give me advice on what to do with my life."

Rowan's expansion on the picture of a life hemmed in by her mother's dominating personality disturbed Nic. It was such a different upbringing from the fortunate one he'd judged it to be. To keep from dwelling on the struggles that pulled far more empathy out of him than he was comfortable with, he focused on her oblique request, touring his father's suite to see if his idea was feasible.

The rooms sprawling from the southwestern turret of the house were befitting of a billionaire media mogul—expansive and masculine, yet with enough womanly touches to prove one had lived here with him. Nic briefly glanced in the walk-in closet, approving of its size, reassured by contents that were even more extravagant than he'd expected. He detoured out of interest to the well-appointed lounge, with its balcony overlooking the sea, noted the his and hers bathrooms and acknowledged the bed—big as the Titanic.

Rowan watched him with an inquisitive frown. "Have you never been in here before?"

"Never. You?"

"Loads," she said with a careless shrug.

Dismissing a weary *of course she had*, he gave the framed portraits a final considering look. "I think you should sell your mother's things and use the money to get a degree in something practical like business admin."

Rowan's love for her mother might be very much of the dutiful variety, and stained with resentment and angst, but she was appalled by Nic's suggestion. "I can't do that!" she protested.

Nic lifted his brows at her vehemence. "Why not?"

"Mum loved this table and that mirror… You can't just tear down someone's life and make it disappear." Her lingering sense of duty to preserve Cassandra O'Brien's mystique made her balk at the idea completely. "And business admin? Why don't you suggest I become an accountant? Or something really exciting like an insurance actuary? Maybe there's a library somewhere that needs its Dewey Decimal System overhauled?"

"Put it all in storage and wait tables, then." A muscle tightened in Nic's jaw, giving Rowan the crazy impression that she'd injured him. "I don't know you any better than you know yourself," he stated, in a comeback that returned very nicely any wounding she'd delivered. "Given what you just said, this is a decision best made by you, isn't it?"

Nic took on his warrior stance, strong and mute. If he wasn't the product of Thor and Athena she didn't know what he was, all masculine power and superiority.

His confident presence called to the woman in her, but his subtext didn't escape her. He wasn't contradicting her need to move on, and his mention of disposing of her mother's things reinforced his expectation that she'd do so.

Taking a surreptitious breath to ease the panicky constriction in her lungs, she nodded, mulling over what he'd said. "You're right. I need to figure it out on my own. But there is one thing we should plan together." She shoved aside the barbed wires curling around the tender walls of her heart to allow the statement out. "We need a memorial service."

He jerked back his head in immediate refusal. "I don't. Why would you?"

"Everyone does." She hugged herself tighter.

"No. It's a social convention that many subscribe to, particularly if they're of a religious bent, but that doesn't mean you and I have to buckle to it."

"It's not buckling! It offers closure." He couldn't really imagine she'd sign a piece of paper and that would be it, could he?

Rowan stared at his impermeable expression and got a sick, hollow feeling in her stomach. She was such an idiot. She had thought sleeping with him would change things. Change *him*. Soften his edges and make him feel…something.

Nic shook his head at Rowan's stare of horrified objection, continually amazed by how sentimental she was. His inner core tightened protectively against that weakness. What was nostalgia but revisiting old pain?

"What did you have in mind? You and I reading poetry to each other over a marker on the lawn?" he asked.

"You don't have to be like that about it!" Her sniff of affront was followed by a haughty set of her chin that made him feel about two inches tall. "I thought we'd say something nice to people who care about them in a chapel in Athens."

"Oh, you want a *party*," he said with sudden realization, disgusted with himself for beginning to credit her with more substance. "Why didn't you say so? *No*."

"It's a service!" Rowan argued. "People need one. Aren't you getting emails and phone calls? Their friends are asking for a chance to pay their respects."

"Which they've done," Nic insisted. If he had to field one more empty platitude or soupy look he'd drop *himself* from a plane into the sea. "There is absolutely no reason to drag it all into the limelight again—or is that your goal? Feeling a bit isolated here, Ro? Then *leave*."

Well, that certainly told her how much he valued their time together! Rowan's belligerent chin took his dismissal as a direct hit, pulling in and—she feared—crumpling before she steadied it.

"Is there really nothing in you that feels a need to say goodbye? Or are you only willing to give Olief as much time as he gave you?" It was a cruel thing to say. He'd spent hours on the search personally, and hiring teams of divers and pilots…

He didn't remind her of all that. He only stared flatly at her. The silence stretched. His stance hardened and his jaw clenched.

Her belly quivered in apprehension.

"I said no." He walked out.

Nic kept his distance for the next several days. If Rowan had lazed around underfoot he might have given her a piece of his mind, but she was actually doing as he'd told her to. She'd made a few trips to the other side of the island to fetch empty boxes. Garment bags had appeared with labels and markers. Every day, when she wasn't leaving him a meal downstairs, she spent hours packing up the master bedroom.

If she had come to *him* he might have engaged, but he would not go looking for her. He was too proud. So proud it made his shoulders ache with hollow pressure. But the way she'd taken everything he'd told her and thrown it back in his face had been a blow. It was a perfect example of why he didn't let people in. He didn't want anyone to have the power to hurt him. If that meant he didn't get the closeness—the sex and laughter and moments of basking in the light of a woman's smile—so be it. Those were things he refused to crave anyway.

And if he had a curious tingling in his chest, almost like he was *missing* her—well, that was pure stupidity. She was right down the hall.

Or was she? He thought he heard a knock and clicked off his shaver.

"Nic?" She was in his lounge. Grabbing a towel off the rail, he hitched it around his hips and pulled the bathroom door inward.

Rowan was halfway around the sofa, heading toward the double doors that led into his bedroom. She started when he revealed himself, visibly taken aback to find him so close and fresh from the shower, but what did she expect at six-thirty in the morning?

She was in a short robe belted loosely over a torturously short babydoll nightgown. Her warm sleep scent, like almonds and tea, teased his nostrils. Despite going months without a woman on many occasions, he suddenly and acutely felt this recent abstinence.

A flustered blush colored her cheeks and she took a half step back, then held her ground within his reach even though he could tell she was discomfited.

Desire pulsed through him with increasing punches from his strengthening heart rate, reacting to her tousled hair and fresh-from-bed look. He wanted to heave her over his shoulder and carry her to his unmade sheets, but alongside his immediate lust was a pang of surprise at how exhausted she looked. Her eyes were green gems in bruised sockets, her skin thin and pale.

He wasn't exactly sleeping well himself. Every day was a fight to incapacitate his sex drive with punishing workouts. Every night he woke to erotic dreams anyway, heavy and aching to go to her.

Funny how there was no satisfaction in knowing she was suffering too. He shifted his weight so his feet were braced wide, hopeful that his uncontrollable response to her wouldn't become obvious.

"Yes?" he demanded.

She swallowed and ran a hand through her hair, reminding him how silky and thick it was, how good it had felt to grasp a handful of the luscious waves and kiss her until neither of them could breathe.

Her breath sucked in and she said in a rush, "I just heard the ferry horn. It's coming now. I totally forgot they change the schedule on weekdays."

His sex thoughts dissipated under something that made him pull inward with apprehension—even though he didn't know why a change in the ferry schedule was such a crisis she had to burst in here, wringing her hands over it. "So?"

"That means I have to pack and leave now, unless you're coming and want to make other arrangements to get us to the city by two."

His brain stalled on *pack and leave*. The rest penetrated more slowly and didn't make a lick of sense. "What?"

Rowan folded her arms across her chest in a move that was so defensive he instinctively knew he didn't want to be enlightened. She spoke with exaggerated patience that annoyed him further.

"I thought I would have more time to reason with you, but I've just realized I don't. I have to go now. Unless you're willing to have the helicopter come and get us in a few hours? In that case we have all kinds of time to fight."

"About…?" He tensed right down to the arches of his bare feet.

Her mouth pursed before she took a brave breath and stated, "The service."

CHAPTER NINE

"WHAT? Service?"

The way Nic chomped the words made Rowan tremble internally, but it was far too late to back down. She'd known as she set this up that the worst part would be now, when she told him—and there had been a lot of hard parts, not least of which had been finding the money. She'd put off telling him as long as she could, avoiding him, checking that he couldn't overhear her calls. All the way along she'd known she'd need to set aside patience and temper to make him see she was doing the right thing.

Now, though, a mental clock ticked in her head. The ferry's horn usually sounded when it reached the tip of the island. It took ages to empty and reload, so she had at least thirty or forty minutes to get to the marina, but she suspected that wouldn't give her enough time to talk Nic around to her way of thinking.

There wasn't enough time in the world for that. If only he wasn't naked and looking like the biggest, angriest Viking ever to rip off his shirt and go berserk.

"I made it clear we weren't holding a service." That low, livid voice nearly made her knees collapse.

"*We* aren't holding one, are we?" She spoke with admirable civility, keeping the quaver out of her voice. "*I* am.

Courtesy demands I invite you. Could you make up your mind? I have to run if you're not coming."

"How could you?" His fingers curled as if he wanted to close them on her neck.

"Option two, then? We're fighting." Her temper caught like a cat's claw. She might have kept her distance while she made the plans, aware that continuing their sexual relationship while going behind his back would make this betrayal worse, but he had completely ignored her for days! That *hurt*. "Or are you literally asking me how I did it? Because I don't need your permission and I have resources."

"Table dancing?" he derided.

"What else?" she taunted to hide the smart. "Of course in order to earn enough to pay for this big *party* I'm hosting I'll have take off my clothes this time."

Outrage arced from him like an electric bolt, making her jerk as he seemed to rise taller and loom over her. "That had better be a lie."

"What's it to you?" she cried, the words coming straight from the forsaken nights that had piled up in the last few days.

This was the hardest time of her life and he was making it harder with his hot and cold attitude, the exquisite peaks of pleasure he'd brought her to and the pit of dejection he'd left her in. Her incendiary anger carried her forward, resentful words charging off her tongue.

"What do you care if I sell myself on street corners and buy gold-plated urns? I'm just a girl you sleep with when you're bored. I don't rate so much as a good morning or a thanks for lunch or a kiss goodnight!"

An inferno of anger roared in his eyes. *Wrong thing to fight about*, she thought, but his rebuff pained her so deeply she couldn't help herself.

"Maybe if you'd spoken to me I might have told you!"

she rushed on, with a contentious lift of her chin, the burn of humiliation searing through her. "But you didn't even invite me for a spin in one of the guest rooms. What's the matter, Nic? Does sleeping with me make you hate me less?"

He caught her by the upper arms before she saw him move. "What do you want from me? Flowers? Romance? *Caring?* Prepare for disappointment. I'm not built that way. But if you're missing the sex keep talking. I'll accommodate you," he warned.

She could have done a million things: said something cruel, sent her knee into his groin. She wasn't scared by his threat, though. She was aroused. So was he. The hectic flush across his cheekbones, the unsteady rise and fall of his chest and the bulge of his towel filled her with euphoria.

He didn't want to want her, though, and that made her mad. It gave her the power to strike back in the one way she knew would completely undermine his control: she whipped off his towel and threw it to the floor.

"Really?" He backed her into the wall, incredulous.

"What are you going to do about it?" she taunted.

His fierce blue eyes never left hers as his hands shot to her waist, brushing open her robe before descending to her bare thighs in a rough caress. His hands climbed to her hips, bunching the hem of her short nightie over his wrists.

She gasped and jerked at his proprietorial touch, shamefully flooding with heated wetness. It had been *days!* His breath left him in a ragged laugh as he realized there were no panties to remove. He reached to cup her buttocks, sliding his palms to the backs of her thighs beneath the curve of her bottom, and lifted her.

She parted her legs in a practiced leap, arms reaching over his bunching shoulders to brace her weight on him. Something brazen and fierce was taking hold in her. A knot of anguished loneliness had been building in her and the only way to break it apart was with the hot penetration of her body by his.

She was completely ready for him, whether from her erotic dreams and constant fantasies or because sexual frustration had been at the heart of this fight in the first place. She didn't know. Only knew that she was wet and needy. And when he embedded himself in her with one smooth thrust she cried out in primal fulfillment, locking her legs around his waist with frantic, brazen determination.

He swore and tried to gentle things. She wouldn't let him. His fingers bit into the backs of her thighs as she engaged every well-trained muscle in her body and let her weight deepen his thrusts. Welling emotion was threatening to overflow in her. She wanted to absorb him completely and nipped at his mouth, holding the sides of his head as she sucked hard on his bottom lip.

He leaned them into the wall and pumped harder. Faster. Making her body clench around him stronger and tighter. The crescendo approached. She clasped him in greedy frenzy, determined to bring him over the edge with her as she felt the rushing expansion, both of them tipping, falling, flying…

Nic felt her climax arrive in a powerful clench that nearly took him alive. He let go with an explosion of molten heat so intense his skin went icy. The backlash of pleasure left him too weak to do anything but pin her to the wall, his hips finishing in uneven thrusts. She shivered around him, wringing magnificent throbs from him as he emptied himself into her. Her moans of rapture filled his mouth like spun sugar.

Drained, he stayed leaning on her for long moments, muscles shaking in strain.

Unprotected sex, he thought dimly, and a craven fear unfurled in him—something so apprehensive and insecure he drew in a sharp breath.

At his sudden inhalation Rowan quit playing her hand softly at the back of his neck. Her touch held a tenderness he'd only recognized when she'd moved her hand to his shoulder in a silent request for release. Another clench of loss hit him.

His head felt too heavy to lift. He didn't want to disengage and experience the rush of cool air between them, or watch her nearly crumple because her legs refused to hold her. Chagrin poured through him as he reached to steady her, disturbed by how she trembled and avoided his gaze. "Rowan—"

"If I miss that ferry I'll never forgive you." There wasn't much snap left in her voice. It was more a statement of fact. Weary resignation.

The service. Infuriated anger bled back, but there wasn't anything he could do. Keeping her from it would only make both of them look bad.

"I'll arrange the chopper." He rubbed his face, already dreading the ordeal, his mind split with anger at her for putting him in this position and a more embryonic profound trepidation. She was at the door before he managed to say, "I didn't use anything."

"I know. The timing's wrong. It's fine."

No, it wasn't. Nothing about what had just happened was *fine*.

So that's how babies are made, Rowan thought as she showered, dazed by the primordial way she and Nic had clashed like two cells intent on comingling their DNA. The fact that pregnancy was impossible should be providing her with a sense of relief, but it only increased the for-lorn feeling of isolation that had been eating her all week.

Was that why she'd provoked him? To force his attention when she had been feeling neglected? She'd been so anxious about the tense distance growing between them. Had she just pulled the oldest trick in the female book? Trying to keep him with sex? Dumb idea. He wouldn't hate her any less for goading him into losing control.

Filled with conflicted disappointment, she stepped out of the shower, thankful she couldn't see her wan reflection in the fogged mirror.

Self-pity is not a good look, as her mother would say. *Men are drawn to confidence.*

Right. She had a performance to get through, she thought with a ripple of misplaced hysterical humor. She reached for her makeup case, determined to hide her pained wistfulness from Nic.

His perfunctory knock a few minutes later shattered her efforts at gathering her composure, but he was only inform-ing her they'd leave as soon as she was ready. "We'll dress at my apartment. I need a suit," he said through the door.

"Okay," she called back.

The impersonal exchange burned from her constricted throat all the way into the pit of her stomach. She'd told him the timing was wrong, but that wasn't true. The body was wrong. Underweight. *Infertile.* Not uncommon in her former world of over-training and under-eating. She had never let it bother her, but it suddenly seemed like one more way she fell short, and that was too much to bear when she already felt like he hated her.

Thankfully, Nic didn't seem to want to talk when she eventually faced him. Locking himself away physically wasn't possible, so he did it mentally, acting like the sex hadn't happened. He hustled her into the helicopter on the lawn and waited until they reached Athens to ask about the service. Where and when was it being held? Who was speaking?

She answered numbly, thinking about how anxious she'd been as she made the arrangements, dreading his anger, dreading attending alone. Now it was overshadowed by a chilly tension that had nothing to do with her going against his wishes.

"I tried to keep the press off the scent," she assured him. "Well, as much as possible when the man owned half the world's papers and news stations."

No smirk, just a tic in his cheek. "And how did you pay for everything?"

It occurred to her he might be doing the same thing she was: talking about the service to avoid dissecting this morning. Or maybe he was satisfied with her answer that the timing was wrong and just wanted the service out of the way and her out of his life.

She swallowed, mentally balancing on that ledge of a week ago, with deadly waves threatening to engulf her and no way to get back to where she'd been.

He was leading her to the guest room in his high-rise penthouse. She craned her neck to orient herself. It was a surprisingly soothing expanse of rooms that flowed one into another, surrounding an outdoor pool and a view of the Parthenon that stole her breath. Rosedale must make him feel hemmed in, she realized, and accepted that she'd never win him over on the mansion. Perhaps she should have listened without judging, because she could stay in a place as private and sunny as this penthouse forever.

"My mother's agent is floating me a loan," she answered absently when she realized he was waiting.

"Introduce me to him. I'll repay him."

Her pride prickled. Hosting a service was her choice.

She wouldn't let it become his problem. "I've got it. It's not like there's caskets and burials."

"It's my responsibility. I'll take care of it."

"You cut me off because you wanted me to show responsibility," she reminded. "Pay half, if you insist, but I refuse to owe you money. I'll keep my loan with Frankie."

"Don't start a fight you can't win, Rowan."

"I'd rather not fight at all."

"That's funny," he said without a shred of humor, and closed the door.

Nursing anger at Rowan for putting him in the position of owing a stranger for the cost of his own father's service kept Nic from brooding on the disquiet eating a hole in his breastbone. It allowed him to lock his emotions so deeply in his personal dungeon he almost forgot what he was dressing for until he walked into the lounge.

Rowan wore a simple black top over a knit black skirt. Slits in the skirt revealed her high boots and black stockings. Her silhouette, graceful as always, was startlingly slight, making his breath catch. A deep purple scarf held her straightened hair so the length lay in a gleaming line down her right shoulder. She clutched a black pocketbook and opened it when he appeared, walking toward him with purpose as she extracted something.

He tensed, anticipating the hint of sexual awareness that always struck with her nearness, and found himself thrust back to their wild copulation in his lounge. Her invitation might have been more of a dare, but she had participated, welcomed him, taken him in like it was as vital to her as it had been to him. It had been raw and primeval and mind-shattering. He'd never wanted or needed anyone like that before. The culmination had been more than physical. It had been spiritual.

And exceedingly careless of him.

She'd said the timing was wrong, but what if it wasn't? What if it was bang on?

His gut was a cement mixer as he stared at the part in her hair, trying to see into the workings of her mind. What if she fell pregnant? What would she do?

His palms began to sweat.

Her subtle scent invaded his dark thoughts, disguised by a designer bouquet of *grigio* citrus, but he detected the almonds and fresh tea, unique as the rest of her. It was a punch of homespun warmth, gentle and feminine and familiar.

He wanted to reach for her, but the last time he'd done that he'd behaved like an animal. It underlined exactly what he'd told her: he was incapable of true caring.

Guilt hardened in him, stiffening his muscles as he waited to see why she had come so close. Searching for a clue to her motive, he noted that the only adornment on her outfit of unrelieved black was a pair of pins above her heart: one a small emerald brooch that formed a lucky four-leaf clover, the other a familiar insignia—the Marcussen Media four-color shield with an inlaid "O" of white gold.

"How is that a pin?" he asked as he recognized Olief's cufflink.

"I sent them out to be converted." Rowan removed the tiepin he was wearing and replaced it with the matching cufflink inlaid with an "M." She took care to ensure it sat straight. Her nearness, the light graze of her touch between the buttons of his shirt, was like a magnetic interference against his invisible force field, making his self-control shiver and threaten to short. The gesture was so simple and inclusive he felt his throat close over any words he might have found to remark on it.

At the same time he was devastated by the familial connection it symbolized. That wasn't him. He'd been rejected as a son. He'd never make a decent father. His lungs shrank and he began to grow cold.

With a critical eye Rowan scanned his appearance, her hands sweeping across his shoulders, smoothing his lapels, adjusting the kerchief poking out of his pocket.

"Don't." He couldn't bear her touch when he felt so raw.

Her gaze came up. Her mouth still looked bruised, and now so did her eyes. Her vulnerability made his gut clench, sending a spike of regret through him. When he ran his tongue behind his lip he could still feel where her teeth had cut in, leaving a taste of rust. She'd been lost in rapture, but his behavior had still been incredibly crass.

Reckless.

She flinched under his scowl and turned away. "I know you think this is just one more selfish act by a spoiled socialite, but I'm doing it for them. Well, maybe a little for myself." She dropped his original tiepin into her pocketbook. "I let Mum down so many times. I need to give her this at least."

The defeat in her was so tangible, his throat ached as she crossed the room away from him.

"I'm not angry about the service," he blurted.

"What, then?" She drew herself to the full extent of her slender height, seeming to brace herself. She knew. She could see the elephant in the room as well as he could. What they'd done this morning shouldn't have happened.

Could she also see how much he hated himself for putting them in this position? That he wanted to lock his arms around her and beg her not to do anything rash? But he knew it would be better to send her away and let her make her own decision, because he could never be the kind of man capable of involving himself with a woman and their child.

Maybe there wasn't even a baby to worry about. She'd said the timing was wrong.

Shades of regret rose in him, but his ingrained hesitation against emotions—experiencing them, labeling them, acting on them—prevented him from examining that.

The intercom buzzed, making them both jump.

"It's just the car," he managed through a dry throat.

Rowan nodded jerkily and shrugged into her coat before he realized what she was doing. He didn't move forward in time to help her and his hand closed on empty air. It stayed locked in a fist that her sharp gaze detected on her way to the door.

"After this I'll finish packing her things and get out. I promise."

The words scooped into his chest, leaving a gaping space in him. *Grief,* he told himself. For the last year he'd taken refuge from it in work or the gym. His refusal to host a service had largely been an attempt to avoid revisiting the loss.

The choke of sorrow and missed chances had moved into the background of his psyche, though. All his tension and misgivings were rooted in Rowan's behavior right now. She was on the run, and he didn't blame her, but it filled him with anxiety.

The elevator floor dropped away from beneath his unfeeling legs and the blurred city passed before his eyes. He could only clench a hand on the nearest surface and try to hold on to his equanimity while trying to convince himself that facing the memorial service was eating him alive. Not something else.

After this I'll finish packing her things and get out.

His cold fog grew worse when the car slowed outside a low building. Nic finally came out of himself long enough to see how gray her complexion had gone, leaving her makeup as slashes of garish color against her waxen face.

"Are you going to throw up?" He reached for the ice bucket.

"It's stage fright." Her shaking hand went to her middle. "I didn't eat, so nothing to toss. It'll go away as soon as I'm on." She left the car like a ghost rising from a grave, her movements elegant as always, her collected expression niggling at him.

Was she really not the least bit worried? If timing was so reliable there wouldn't be an overpopulation problem. Or had she already made a decision that a baby *wouldn't* happen, no matter what?

He took Rowan's elbow as they climbed the stairs, consciously easing a grip that wanted to tighten with urgency. His heart pounded. *Don't, Rowan. Please don't.*

People were already seated inside—hundreds of them. Once they sat, a man in robes invited them to bow their heads. It was surreal, given his state of mind, but cleansing. This *was* the right thing to do. He should have known, should have trusted that Rowan understood these things better than he did.

As she moved to the podium a few minutes later he noted that she had regained some color, but her eyes were still too big for her face. He watched her with a fatalistic rock in his chest. She was so much better than he was, rising above a difficult childhood like a phoenix, able to sing her mother's praises, warm and beautiful, while he carried only the ashen darkness of his childhood with him, staining everything black.

He had nothing to offer a woman and a child but the same bleak void he'd grown up in. Making her pregnant would be a disaster. He had no choice but to pray it wouldn't happen, yet a torturous want crowded into him.

A deep, undeniable ache filled him to be better than he was. Damn Olief for never setting an example or instilling confidence in him when it came to interpersonal relationships. He'd left his son floundering, armed only with a shaky desire to succeed without any skills to back it up.

Rowan's eyes met his as he struggled with his need to be everything his own father wasn't. Her voice cracked and her hand came up to cover her trembling lips. Her self-possession began to fall apart and threatened to shatter Nic's. Purely out of instinct he pushed to his feet, moving to stand beside her. It was like stepping into cold fire. He hadn't meant to put himself in this position. Public speaking didn't bother him, but this was different. He never put his emotions on display, and his intense feelings were just under the surface while a sea of faces stared.

He took Rowan's hand. It was so icy his heart tripped in concern. He closed his fingers tightly over hers. She pointed to a place on the page and he began to read.

"'Olief tried hard to be a father figure to me…'" he began, the words evaporating on his tongue. Olief *had* tried with Rowan, and maybe that was the takeaway lesson. He had to say goodbye to Olief's failings as a father and look forward with his own purpose and approach and simply *try*.

Rowan squeezed Nic's hand with all her might, fighting back the breakdown that had come down on her like an avalanche when she had met Nic's tormented gaze. He was genuinely worried she'd turn out to be pregnant. She'd seen it back at the apartment, had even tried to brace herself for reassuring him how remote a possibility it was, but dread turned like a medieval torture device in her. He'd be relieved and she would be crushed.

The arrival of the car had saved her, but as she'd stood up here, playing the part of the good daughter, all she'd been able to think was that it was her mother's fault she had no periods. Even before the intensity of ballet classes the pressure had been on to mind her calories. Rowan had felt like a hypocrite, talking up the woman she resented deep in her heart. Then she'd looked into Nic's eyes and known he didn't want her to conceive, and with equal fervor knew she wished she *could*.

Yet wouldn't.

It had been too much, and she was clinging to composure by her fingernails.

Nic closed with a few personal words of his own, Rowan swallowed, and thankfully they were able to sit down. But Nic didn't let go of her hand. Maybe that was her fault. Her fingers were white where she entwined them with his. She stared at their linked frozen hands as one of her mother's friends rose to sing an Irish ballad.

The worst was over. She only had to get through the reception in the adjoining hall without betraying her inner tension. As they stood to move through the doors that were thrown open for them she disengaged from Nic's grip. "You don't have to stay," she offered, even though he'd said he wasn't angry about the service anymore.

His dark brows came down like storm clouds, scolding and chilly. "I'll stay."

She felt a lash of fear. A wild impulse to bolt from here whirled through her. *Very mature, Ro.* But there was something resolved in his expression. She sensed a *Talk* looming and wasn't prepared to face it.

"Suit yourself," she murmured, and let herself be drawn by people who were anxious to express their condolences.

Nic wondered if he had imagined her clammy grip on his hand. She was so willing to have him disappear now. Because she blamed him? She had every right. He was the experienced one—in more ways than one. He shouldn't have taken such a risk with her.

He wished it was as simple as saying she had provoked him, but that wasn't right. Hearing she'd been hurt by his neglect had rattled him. *"Maybe if you'd spoken to me..."* But he'd been afraid to speak to her, afraid she would hurt him again with all that he'd told her. He hadn't liked facing that he was a coward who had avoided her out of fear.

"Does sleeping with me make you hate me less?"

Yes, it did. Which scared him even more and made him profoundly aware of his inability to love. He'd said something crude at that point, infuriated that he could never be what she needed and deserved. The futility of their relationship had struck home and he'd wanted quite desperately, just for a second, to bind her to him in the most irrevocable way possible.

He watched her work the room filled with screen stars, diplomats, business magnates and overgrown titled children. For the first time he didn't see a spoiled girl demanding attention. He saw a young woman who ensured everyone was noticed, greeting individuals affectionately and putting them at ease.

He did his duty, distantly thanking people for coming, but he couldn't help acknowledging what a perfect foil Rowan made for his innately brisk demeanor, brimming with natural warmth and beauty. If their lives became bound by a child—

He refused to let the thought progress, still disturbed by the near yearning he'd felt as he'd contemplated becoming a father while saying goodbye to his own. He tracked down Franklin Crenshaw instead, waiting out the requisite expression of sympathy before nodding at the elegance of the wine and cheese reception.

"I appreciate all you've done. Please send me the bills."

Frankie shook his head. "Rowan made all the arrangements. I only opened an account for her." A rueful smile twitched the man's lips. "But I'm not surprised she's asked you to settle up for her. She doesn't want to owe me, does she?"

Nic slipped into his investigative reporter guise. "Why do you say that?"

"Because she knows how I'll ask her to repay me."

"She can't dance," Nic asserted, instantly protective of her injured leg.

"No, but she can act. Look at her. What a way to spend your birthday," Frankie said under his breath, stealing a glass of wine from a passing tray.

The date struck Nic like a bludgeon, taking his disgraceful behavior this morning to a new realm of discredit. *"Never a good morning or a thank you..."* His insides clenched against more evidence that he failed at interpersonal relationships.

"She's hanging by a thread," Frankie said with pained admiration. "No one else sees it, but when that girl can't find a smile you know she's on her last nerve."

Nic took it as judgment. *He* was the reason her stress level was through the roof.

"I bet she hasn't eaten either," Frankie mused.

With a soft curse, Nic excused himself.

Rowan was wrung out by the time they returned to Nic's suite. She could barely unzip her boots and pull them off her aching feet.

Nic shrugged out of his suit jacket, then poured two drinks—brandy, she assumed. He brought them to her and she did what she had done with the coffee, tea, and plates of food he'd handed her throughout the long day. She set it down on the nearest surface.

He sighed.

"Don't be mad, Nic. I can't do it," she said lifelessly.

"I'm not mad, but we have to talk."

"Not now. I just want this day to be over." She saw him wince, and regretted being so blunt, but the service had been hard enough without the undercurrents between them. He'd never left her side and she was at the end of her rope. "I'm going to bed."

Nic picked up her untouched drink as she walked away, considering going after her. But why? So they could continue battling to keep their emotions in check? He was done with crumpled tissues and weepy embraces. His wall of imperviousness couldn't stand another hit. Ro had it right. Finish the day and start fresh tomorrow.

But his tension wouldn't ease until they'd talked through the various scenarios and how they'd react to them. He couldn't imagine sleeping with so much on his mind and resented her for dragging this out. How could she be so calm about it? Didn't she realize what was at stake? That their lives could be changed forever?

Look who he was dealing with, though. Rowan was the first to turn anything into a joke.

Frustrated, he carried his drink in one hand and tugged at his tie with the other, heading for his bedroom and a fruitless try at sleeping. As he passed Rowan's door he heard a noise. A deep, wrenching sob.

His heart stalled, then kicked in with a painful downbeat. Filled with dread, he slowly pushed the door open. She sat on the side of the bed, one arm out of her shirt, the fabric bunched around her torso as she rocked, keening, her face buried in her white hands.

The jagged pressure that swelled behind his sternum threatened to clog his lungs. Something between an instinct and a memory pushed him further into the room, even though his feet had gone so cold he couldn't feel them.

He set aside the glass and touched her arm. "Ro, stop."

She clutched at him, face running with makeup. "I'm trying," she choked. "But nothing will ever be the s-same again…"

Her distress threatened his shaky control, urging him to run before his defenses fell completely, but he couldn't leave her like this. *Actress*, he thought and felt like a heel for thinking she wasn't affected by all that had happened today. Of course she was. Beneath the beautiful armor and impudent wit was a scared kid who kept taking on more responsibility than was hers to carry.

It struck him that he'd taken advantage of her when he took her to bed. She'd been at a very weak moment in her life. This was why she'd given herself to him. She was losing the life she'd known and now faced even bigger changes.

"It's okay," he lied, brushing away her ineffectual hands, desperate to sop up his guilt. He never should have touched her. He smoothed her hair, releasing the scarf when he came to it. "You're going to be okay, Ro." His shoulders throbbed with remorse. He stripped her to her undies and eased her beneath the sheet, desperate to tuck her in and close this day for her.

Tomorrow they'd talk. What he needed now was time to come to terms with the injury he'd done her if he'd got her pregnant.

"Don't leave, Nic, please," she pleaded, pressing his fingers to her soaked cheek.

He wavered. She was an iceberg. He compromised by toeing off his shoes and dragging his belt free one-handed, remaining clothed as he moved under the covers. With a tight embrace he tried to keep her shuddering frame from falling apart.

"Just until I fall asleep," she murmured. "Then you can go. I'm sorry."

"No, *I'm* sorry," he said with deep anguish, and soothed the fresh tension that gathered in her. "Shh. Go to sleep. It'll be okay," he lied again, while the possibility of an unplanned pregnancy circled in his mind like a shark's fin. "You'll see."

CHAPTER TEN

Rowan stretched and the hot weight of blankets surrounding her moved.

When she opened her eyes Nic's arresting blue eyes were right there, hooded and enigmatic, fixed on hers. His jaw was smudged with a night's growth of bronze-gold stubble, his hair glinting in the morning sunlight pouring through the uncovered window.

Her breakdown last night came back to her in a rush. The day had been an endurance event of fielding enquiries about her leg and her future. She didn't have any pat answers, and through it all Nic had loomed over her like a giant microscope, seeming to watch her every move.

The tension hadn't let up, so it was understandable that after holding them back all day she had let her emotions get the better of her when she was finally alone. Letting Nic find her at such a low point and grasping at him like a lifeline, however, made her feel more raw and exposed than after the wicked things they'd done to each other in the throes of passion.

Flinching in vexation, she sat up to let her hair curtain her face while she tried to minimize how defenseless she felt. "Gosh, was that *your* virginity I just took? I can't imagine you've spent many nights fully clothed in bed with a female without the precursor of sex. Be honest—not counting this one, how many?"

"She's back," he remarked under his breath, pushing away the covers and rolling to sit on the far edge of the bed. "As it happens, you're not my first," he stated flatly. "I used to let my baby sister snuggle up to me when she'd had a bad dream."

Rowan stared at the wrinkled back of his shirt, barely able to process the information through her sleep-muddled brain. "You have a *sister*? But you said— On your mother's side? Is she younger?"

"And two half-brothers, if you're taking a tally."

No surprise to learn he was the oldest, but the rest stunned her. "That's a big family. Why do you never talk about them?"

His shoulders jerked, then he stood abruptly. Maybe she'd imagined his flinch.

"I don't talk *to* them." He stretched his arms toward the ceiling and his shirt came loose from his waistband while his joints cracked. "My aunt used to bring us together for a week in the summer when she lived in Katarini, but once she moved to America my mother's husband put a stop to my seeing them. He didn't like them coming home and talking about me."

"That's mean!" Rowan's already peeled-thin heart was abraded further by his casual reference to what amounted to outright cruelty. "Your poor mother," she couldn't help adding, sitting in the pool of rumpled blankets and retrospective empathy.

"My poor *mother*?" Nic swung around with a harsh expression of astonishment, arms lowering.

"Well, yes." Rowan shrugged, her hand imperceptibly tightening on the edge of the sheet. "Having to stay married to someone like that. He's probably the reason she didn't see you at school. He sounds controlling."

"She didn't 'have to' stay married to him. She *chose* to. She chose him over me." His flash of rejection was quick and deep, so swiftly snatched back and hidden behind chilling detachment she could only guess how much practice he'd had at stifling it.

Rowan's heart, ravaged by all that had happened in the last week, finished rending in two. She ached to offer him one of those ragged halves, the one beating at a panicky pace, but doubted he'd take it. No wonder he held himself at such a distance. Distance was all he'd been taught.

There weren't any platitudes that could make up for what had been done to him, so she tried to offer perspective.

"What other choice did she have?" she asked gently. "She already had your sister and the boys."

"One boy. She was pregnant with the other," he admitted, one hand rasping his stubbled jaw as though he wanted to wipe away having started this conversation.

"There you go. How does a woman with three children and about to give birth to a fourth hold down a job? Who nurses that baby while she's at work? It sounds like her choices came down to destroying the lives of all her children or just one. I'm not saying she made the right choice, but I don't think she had any good ones. It was an awful position to be in."

"She could have chosen not to get into that position. She married knowing I was on the way." His eyes were so dark they were nearly black. "She could have broken her engagement and asked Olief to support her. For that matter, given they were both committed elsewhere, they never should have made me in the first place!"

Suppressing a stark pang of protest against his never being born, Rowan only said, "Because every pregnancy is planned?" She choked that off, appalled she'd started to go there. She only wanted him to see everyone was human. "It happens, Nic," she rushed on, fixing her gaze blindly on the blurred pattern of the curtains. "Sometimes the choices you're left with are tough ones. Judging by your reaction to my efforts toward you, you're not interested in having a family, so what would *you* do?" she challenged with a spurt of courage. "Marry me anyway?"

It was a less than subtle plea for him to qualify his feelings toward her. He'd been so solicitous, holding her close all night. It made her heart well with hope that something deeper between them was possible.

He'd hardened into something utterly rigid, utterly unyielding. When he spoke, his voice was coated in broken glass. "The greater question is what would *you* do?"

His chilly withdrawal made her insides shrink. She wasn't sure how to interpret his grim question, but his quiet ferocity gave her a shiver of preternatural apprehension. She was convinced he didn't want her to be pregnant, so was he hoping to hear she wouldn't go through with it? He would be vastly disappointed! Her heart hardened like a shield inside her. *Nothing* would make her give up her baby.

"It would be beyond a miracle if I got pregnant so I'd keep it, of course. But don't worry," she charged with barely restrained enmity. "I wouldn't ask you to marry me. My mother's shotgun marriage ruined her life. I'll never repeat *that* mistake."

She threw off the blankets and locked herself in the bathroom, shaken to the bone. She tried to regain control by reminding herself they were arguing about something that couldn't even happen, but when she stood in the shower a few minutes later her hand went to her abdomen where a hollow pang of *if only* throbbed.

* * *

"I'd keep it, of course."

There was no "of course" about it, but Nic was reassured that Rowan had said it. Which was crazy. The thought of making a baby with her should be putting him into a cold sweat.

He shifted in the back of the car. He had decided years ago not to have children. Partly it stemmed from spending years in Third World countries. After seeing children savaged by war and famine, their parents helpless to protect or provide for them, he'd concluded that reproducing was irresponsible.

An even deeper resistance came from his certainty that he wasn't built for family life. Every time he'd had the hint of one it had been stripped away—most recently when Olief had flown into that storm. Nic didn't buy into fate, but it really didn't seem he was meant to lead the life of a domesticated man. He'd always been comfortable in that belief. What kind of father would he make anyway, incapable as he was of emotional intimacy?

Rowan would be a good mother, though. Her view of pregnancy was a bit romantic, but it thawed the frozen places inside him. He was reassured. Rowan would show him the way. She was affectionate and playful and knew how to love. His baby would be in good hands because she would love her child even if it *was* his.

The thought caught him by the heart and squeezed. It was such a tiny lifeline, thrown down a well—something delicate and ephemeral in dark surroundings. He wasn't completely sure he'd discerned it. He didn't even have the emotional bravery to reach out and see if it was real. It might not hold. But he wanted to believe it was there.

He glanced at Rowan, his ambivalence high. She'd accused him of not wanting a family and he didn't, he assured himself quickly. The weight of responsibility, the vastness of the decisions and accommodations, were more than he could take. And winding through that massive unknown was a dark line, a fissure. *Him.* The unknown. The weakness. Could he hold a family together or would he be the reason it fell apart?

At the same time he was aware of his heart pounding with… God, was it anticipation? No. He tried to ignore the nameless energy pulsing in him, but he couldn't shake the urge to push forward into the future and see, know, *feel* a sense of belonging after so many years of telling himself to forget what he barely remembered.

He and Rowan were both on their own and surprisingly good together in some ways. He couldn't help wondering if that could extend to parenting a child, making a life together. He could easily stomach waking every morning the way he had today, recognizing Rowan's scent before he opened his eyes. Something had teased at him as he had become aware of her warmth and weight against him. Something optimistic and peaceful. Happiness?

Whatever it was it wouldn't happen, he acknowledged darkly. Her hot statement about shotgun marriages being a mistake had spelled that out clearly enough. She was right; they *were* a mistake. He couldn't even argue that he was good husband material. But her flat refusal to consider marrying him still put a tangle of razor wire in his chest.

She noticed his attention and her hand went to her middle. "Sorry," she said.

They were halfway to the helipad. It took him a second to realize she wasn't referencing a possible baby forming inside her. Her stomach was growling.

"You *still* haven't eaten?"

"You said the car was ready."

"Ready whenever *you* were," he corrected, biting back a blistering lecture on taking care of herself and any helpless beings she might be carrying. "You're a menace," he muttered, and leaned forward to instruct his driver that they were detouring for brunch.

Minutes later they were sitting *al fresco* in the weak winter sun, a little chilly, but blessedly private away from the bustle of hungry diners. He'd ordered a yogurt and fruit cup for Rowan to eat immediately and a proper entrée for each of them to follow.

"I won't get through more than the fruit cup," Rowan warned.

"I'm hungry enough to eat whatever you don't."

"You didn't eat breakfast either? Menace!"

She had her finger hooked in a wedding ring on a delicate chain around her neck. Her mouth twitched behind the back and forth movement as she rolled the ring along its chain. He was inordinately relieved to see the return of her cheeky smile, but still exasperated.

"I'm not eating for two, am I?" he challenged.

She sobered. "Neither am I." She dropped the ring behind her collar.

"You don't know that."

A belligerently set chin and a silent glare was her only reply.

Time would tell, he supposed, dredging up patience, but his hand tightened into an angst-ridden fist. The knife in his belly made a cold, sickening turn as he recalled her rejection of marriage. He steeled himself against the rebuff and ground out, "Yes, by the way, I *would* marry you."

His begrudging statement made Rowan feel like he'd shaken out a trunk of golden treasures and brilliant riches at her feet. But it was all glass and plastic. All for show, with no true value. Numbness bled through her so she barely heard the rest of what he said.

"Don't think for a minute I'd refuse to be part of my child's life."

A choke of what felt like relief condensed in her throat. She wasn't sure why hearing he would be a dedicated parent turned her insides to mush. Maybe because it was a glimmer of the diamond inside the rough exterior. Potential.

She swallowed, but the thorny ache between her breasts stayed lodged behind her sternum. It didn't matter what Nic was capable of if fatherhood was forced upon him. It wouldn't happen. Not with her

Their dishes arrived and she manufactured a weak smile for the waiter, but couldn't unlock her fingers and pick up her utensils.

"I didn't realize your parents were married," Nic said. "Why do you use your mother's name?"

"So no one would find out Mum was married." Her voice sounded a long way off even to her own ears. All she could think was that keeping her mother's secret had been one more accommodation to an overbearing woman whose constant nagging for results had put Rowan in this position: up for the part of Nic's wife and yet not quite qualified.

She ought to tell him she couldn't conceive, but everything in her cringed from admitting it. Even though she could live without making babies. There were other options if she wanted children. She knew that. It was the fact she would never have children with *him* she wasn't ready to admit aloud.

"Is your father alive? Do you see him?" he asked.

Why were they talking about her father? "Yes, of course." Rowan picked up her spoon so she could fill her mouth with yogurt and end that subject.

"Who was he? Why did their marriage put you off it? Was he abusive?"

"Not at all!" Rowan swallowed her yogurt and sat back, surprised Nic would leap to such a conclusion. Perhaps she'd been vehement about what a mistake her parents' marriage had been, but that was how her mum had always framed it. "No, he's just a painter. An Italian."

"So you're not completely without family?" Nic sat back too, wearing his most shuttered expression, not letting her read anything into his thoughts on this discovery.

Rowan licked her lips and her shoulders grew tense. "True. But…um…he's an alcoholic. Not that that makes him less family," she rushed on. "I only mean he's not exactly there for me."

Her helpless frustration with her father's disease reared its head. She rarely mentioned him to anyone, always keeping details vague and hiding more than she revealed. Nic understood that relationships with your father could be complicated, though. That gave her the courage to continue.

"He's an amazing artist, but he doesn't finish much. He's broke most of the time. Olief knew I bought him groceries out of my allowance and paid his rent. He didn't mind. Nic, that's why I did that club appearance. With my leg and everything I hadn't seen my father much, and when I got there—"

She took a deep breath, recalling the smell, the vermin that had taken up residence in his kitchen. Setting down her spoon, she tucked her hands in her lap, clenching them under the table, managing to keep her powerless anger out of her voice.

"It seemed harmless—just one more party and for a good cause." Her crooked smile was as weak as her rationalization had been. "Afterward I realized how easily I could spiral into being just like him and I decided to come back to Rosedale to regroup. I wasn't dancing on tables so I could buy Italian fashions. He needed help."

"You said the marriage ruined your mother's life, but it sounds like it affects you more than it ever did her."

His quiet tone of empathy put a jab in her heart.

"Well, he was my father regardless, and he would have needed my help with or without the marriage. And I do love him even though things are difficult," she pointed out earnestly. "I'm not put off by marriage because he has a drinking problem. Mum just always regretted letting him talk her into making me legitimate, leaving her trapped when she wanted to marry the man she really loved. It made me realize you need more reason to marry than a baby on the way. You need deep feelings for the other person."

His gaze flicked from hers, but not before she glimpsed something like defeat in his blue eyes. Regret. His head shook in subtle dismissive negation—some inner conclusion of dismayed resignation.

A thin sheet of icy horror formed around her heart as she realized she had admitted to wanting to marry for love. There was no shame in it, but she dropped her gaze, appalled that he had read the longing in her and now his hand was a balled up fist of resistance on the tabletop. Everything in his still, hardened demeanor projected that he couldn't do it. Would never love her.

Rowan hadn't imagined he loved her, but confronting the fact that he considered it impossible had her biting back a gasp of humiliation. She blinked hard to push back tears of hurt.

The waiter arrived with their entrées, providing a much needed distraction as he poured coffee and enquired after their needs. At the same time more diners decided to brave the gusting war of spring and winter breezes, taking a table nearby.

They finished their meal in silence.

Nic had locked up when they'd left, so Rowan dug her key from her purse as they came off the lawn from the helicopter pad. She supposed even this quaint touch that her mother had insisted upon—a real key—would go the way of the dodo in whatever high-tech mansion Nic had built.

They stepped into the foyer and both let out a sigh of decompression. Rowan quirked a smile, but the key in her hand dampened her ironic amusement. The jagged little teeth might as well be sawing a circle around her heart. She rubbed her thumb across the sharp peaks, then worked the key off its ring before she lost her nerve.

"What's this?" Nic asked as she left it on the hall table and started up the stairs.

He stood below her, offering her a height advantage she never usually had over him. His thick hair was spiked up in tufts by the wind they'd left outside. She itched to lean down and smooth it.

"I won't need it after I leave." She *had* to leave. She accepted that now. She looked up the stairs, her mind already jumping back into sorting her mother's things. Better that than hanging on to adolescent dreams that could never come true. Nic would never love her. She even understood why he was incapable of it. It was time to move on, no matter how hard and scary.

"Rowan."

His tone stopped her, commanding yet not entirely steady. Height disadvantage or not, he still had the benefit of innate power and arrogance. He still managed to take her breath away with the proud angling of his head.

But an uncharacteristic hesitancy in his expression caused her to tense instinctively.

"If you were pregnant…" he began.

She didn't want this conversation, and tightened her lips to tell him so, but then she realized what he was intimating. She flicked her gaze from the muscle that ticked in his cheek to the bronze key he pinched in his sure fingers.

She felt the blood leave her face. Light-headed, she clung to the rail, trying to hang on to her composure, but it was too cruel of him to hinge keeping her home on something completely impossible.

"If I'm pregnant…what?" Despair gave way to pained affront. The high-ceilinged entryway exaggerated the quaver in her voice with a hollow echo. "I can have Rosedale as a push present? I'm not pregnant, okay? I *can't* get pregnant!"

CHAPTER ELEVEN

THE key in Nic's fist was hot as a bullet he'd snatched from the air to prevent it lodging in his chest. It was circling from another direction to make a precise hit anyway. His upper body was one hard ache of pressure as Rowan ran up the stairs.

He took a step, helpless to call her back when words were backed up in his throat behind shock. His foot caught on their bags and he stumbled. His legs became rubber, clumsy, and started to give out. He sank onto the stairs, elbows on his knees, and pressed the knuckles of his hard fists into his aching eye sockets.

Had he really let himself think it could happen? He was a fool! Of course it wasn't meant to be if it was for him. His insides knotted in a tangle of sick disillusionment.

He swallowed, his chest so hollow it felt like a gaping wound had been cleaved into it. His reaction was as much a sucker punch as the news. When had he started to care?

He *hurt* for Rowan. For a second, as her defenses had fallen away and she had let him see to the bottom of her soul, she'd revealed such a rend in her soft heart...

The urge to go after her drummed in him. But what could he do about something as absolute and irreparable as infertility?

He rubbed his numb face, dragging at the torn edges

of his control. He was fine with not getting the things that meant something to others. Mostly fine. He knew how to live with it. But it gutted him that Rowan, who openly yearned for a proper family, should be denied something that was such a perfect fit for her. He wished…

But he knew better than to wish.

Slowly he stood and climbed the stairs, every joint rusted and stiff. His goal was the sanctuary of his office and work, but he found himself walking past it like a zombie. He followed noises down the hall beyond the open door to Rowan's suite. The double doors to the master bedroom were thrown open and Rowan was taping a box propped on the bed.

She paused briefly when he appeared, just long enough to betray that she'd noted his appearance before she continued screeching the tape gun.

Nic took in the disarray. Boxes were stacked against the walls. Photographs and knickknacks were moved or had disappeared. He didn't care what she was taking. He didn't have any attachment to any of it. But it hit him how many decisions he'd burdened her with. She was a sentimental little thing. She wore a cheap wedding ring that had sealed an unwanted marriage, for God's sake. Digging through all this couldn't be easy for her. What had seemed like the right thing to do suddenly seemed wrong. Unkind.

He wondered if it was his imagination that she looked as if she'd lost weight since yesterday. It might be the baggy T-shirt over braless breasts, but she looked incredibly slight and fragile.

She set down the tape gun and moved to the corner near the balcony. "Did you know Olief was planning an autobiography?" Her sunny tone sounded forced as she pulled the lid off a box and retrieved a packet of yellowed letters. "These are to his wife, talking about the places he was in. There are other things. Photos, awards, columns. It's interesting stuff."

She held out the letters but Nic didn't take them. All his focus was on Rowan. She was so on edge the air was sharp. Her flash of wary vulnerability when she met his gaze was quickly tucked away as she replaced the letters in the box and closed the lid.

"I thought it might give you a better understanding of who he was," she said with stiff consideration and a never-mind shrug.

Part of him was curious. Of course he was. And he could tell that in offering this up she was looking for a measure of forgiveness. It seemed so unnecessary now. She wasn't the reason he had failed to form bonds with Olief. *He* was. Olief had reached out countless times. Nic had always held himself just beyond touching distance.

He scowled as that hard truth sank like talons into his chest. He didn't know how to be there for someone. He'd never wanted to know because no one had been there for him. So what had he thought to accomplish by coming in here? Raking her delicate heart over the smoldering coals of her lost dream of a family?

The inadequacy that had been smoldering in *him* since she'd admitted she wanted to marry for love licked at him with thicker flames.

"It made me realize I should do the same for Mum," she was saying with a jerky nod at the boxes against the far wall. "Giving all that over to a writer would solve a huge problem I have with what to do with playbills and photos of her with other celebrities—"

"I didn't come in here to take book pitches," he said quietly.

"Well, I don't want to talk about what you did come to talk about, so tell me you'll do it or I'll give it to the competition." Her voice was flat, her spine like a thread of glass—deceptively stiff but innately brittle. "Proceeds to benefit a search and rescue foundation, I think, don't you?"

For a second he knew what other people saw when they looked at him: absolute disengagement. His heart gave a vicious twist inside his chest. He *hated* talking about the failed dreams that lived next to his bones. How could he ask her to show him hers? But he had to know more. He lifted a helpless open palm.

"I had no idea, Ro." It astounded him that he hadn't known. Yes, he might have kept his distance from her through the years, but his ears had always been open, his brain quick to store the tidbits he'd gleaned from Olief. "Did Olief know? Did your mum?"

Rowan's chin jutted out stubbornly in profile before he saw her composure crack with a spasm of pain. She turned away to pick up a handtowel grayed with streaks of dust and wiped her fingers on it.

Rowan couldn't believe she'd blurted out the truth so indelicately. Her stomach was still spinning like a bicycle wheel, burning at the edges when she tried to slow it down. She wanted to make some comment like her sterility didn't matter, but her lungs were wrapped in a tight spool of cord.

"Mum didn't think it was a big deal," she finally managed. She looked through the French doors, beyond the balcony, out to the beach. The tide was receding, leaving kelp on the dark, flat sand. Puffy clouds on the horizon promised a breathtaking sunset. *Thanks, Mum. I didn't get what you wanted and I don't get what I want either.*

"Not a big—? Rowan, what happened?" Nic's tone was outraged, but also bewildered. Worried. Closer.

Rowan's pulse sped up, but she didn't let herself turn around and read anything into his nearness or concern.

With great care she folded the towel, even though it would only be thrown down the laundry chute.

"It's not uncommon for women who don't have much body fat to lose their periods," she said, smoothing the blue nap of the towel. "I haven't had one in years. I've gained a little weight since leaving school, but not enough for things to become normal. It might not ever happen."

She was proud of her steady tone, but his silence encased her organs in ice.

"Mum said kids would ruin my career anyway. I guess I thought she was right. That if I was training and working and traveling I wouldn't make much of a mother anyway. So it was for the best." The words burned like a hot iron rod from the back of her throat to the pit of her stomach. "I didn't let myself think of it much at all, to tell the truth. It was too big and—well, you know how doctors are. Quick to blame me because I wasn't taking care of myself. I felt responsible, but also like I couldn't change anything given the pressure I was under, so I ignored it. But with dance no longer being a part of my life and Mum and Olief gone…"

She sighed and the weight on her chest settled deeper.

"…I'm realizing that I would like a family."

She couldn't help the yearning in her voice. This was the first time in her life that she knew what she wanted, deep down and without a doubt. A blanket of calm settled on her. Not peace. Not relief. She knew she wouldn't *get* what she wanted—not the way she wanted it—but at least she knew what would fulfill her. The relief from fruitless searching allowed her to find a smidge of courage and acceptance.

"Some day," she emphasized with a glance over her shoulder.

A light flush warmed her chest and moved outward to her fingertips. A poignant burn chased it. This was the kind of conversation a couple with a future had, but she didn't want Nic thinking she was begging for one.

"Eventually," she insisted, certain she'd revealed too much as she hugged the towel she held. She tried to cover her tracks and self-protect with a hurried, "When the time and the man are right. Obviously I'm not ready now. I've spent all my life pleasing my mother and I'm still responsible for my father. You've said yourself that I'm immature. I can't even take care of myself. I don't have a home or a job…" She stopped, in danger of sounding pitiful. "And it's not like you want me to be pregnant, is it?" She mustered fake cheer as she made herself face him. "Sure, you would have made the best of it, but do you even *want* children?"

A cold sweat broke out on Nic's spine. Rowan had turned the tables so easily. One minute invoking his deepest empathy, the next putting him on the spot with eyes like deep green velvet, pale cheeks like wind-hollowed snow drifts and a wispy smile of brave fatalism softening her mouth. What heartaches did *he* harbor? she asked so ingenuously.

How could he admit that he would have welcomed a baby with her? It would be brutally hurtful, given what she'd just revealed. And unwelcome. *"When the time and the man are right."* A serrated knife of guilt turned in his gut at how comfortable he would have been trapping her to him. *Him.* A man who could never make any woman happy, least of all one who had been unfairly tied down for too long.

"*Do* you want children?" she asked, her lips barely moving while a horrified shadow of inadequacy condensed in her eyes.

He'd hesitated too long. She was reading his silent torment and coming up with failure on her part. What could he do except offer up the agonizing truth? His jaw opened, but his vocal cords were too thick. His hand turned ineffectually for a second before sound finally emerged from his throat.

"I thought it might be a…second chance." A satanic claw reached out and curled piercing talons into his heart, crushing the organ that had grown tender under Rowan's influence. He instantly wished he hadn't said that. A *second* chance? That was not how it worked. You didn't reinvent your own childhood through your offspring.

"What do you mean?" The dark arches of Rowan's brows slanted into a peak of confused hurt. "A second chance for who? At what?"

Was that tentative *hope* in her eyes?

He couldn't examine it, because this was the foggy morning at boarding school all over again. After this, after Rowan had looked right into him, she'd see what everyone but he saw—the lack. The flaw that had made him a child to be turned from without looking back. He swallowed.

"A second chance for me," he admitted, cringing at how pathetic that sounded. "At having a family."

She looked as bloodless as he felt.

He shook his head in slow negation, all sensation falling away as a rushing sound invaded his ears. "I was fooling myself."

"That's not true, Nic—" Rowan started forward but he froze, lifting hands to ward her off, unwilling to have her touch him when he felt so skinless.

The way Nic threw up a wall of resistance, looking utterly rigid, like a block of stone, stopped Rowan in her tracks. She flashed back to the way he'd clamped down on his wistful sadness when talking of his siblings that morning and her heart tipped out of balance on a hard *oh*. How had she ever thought Nic was detached? He was the opposite. His emotions were so scythe-like he couldn't bear to experience them.

"It doesn't matter," he asserted.

The backs of her eyes began to sting. She hated herself then for working her body into sterility. For provoking him into unprotected sex and letting him think briefly that she could give him what he needed. She *never* could.

A terrifying bleakness filled her. If he had loved her they might have found a workaround on making a family together, but there was absolutely no hope for a future with him now.

Rowan ducked her head and brushed a strand of hair back from her face, revealing a porcelain cheek locked in a paroxysm of disorientation and panic.

What must she be thinking? Nic wondered. That she was relieved not to be saddled with an emotional derelict? That she'd had a lucky break? That what he'd revealed made her so uncomfortable she wanted him out of her space?

"I know I'm not like other people," he said, trying to gloss over his confiding something so personal and implausible. "I observe life. I don't participate in it. Yes, I would try to make the best of things, but my best isn't good enough. Any child I created would only suffer and turn out like me. Emotionally sterile."

"No, Nic. That's not true…"

He rejected her outreached hand with an averting of his head. Her shoulders were sinking in defeat and he wanted to pull her softness into him, beg her to fix the broken spaces in him, but he knew enough about relationships to know that was not what you asked of another person. You didn't burden them with fulfilling you. Either you came into the relationship whole and able to offer something to build on, or you did the right thing and walked away, leaving them intact.

"I should get back to work," he said.

When Rowan didn't say anything he glanced at her.

She was staring with wide eyes, her lips pale in a kind of shock. Finally she offered up a barely perceptible, "Me, too."

He made himself leave, but felt her gaze follow him all the way down the hall.

"You're saying Legal is holding you up?" Nic paraphrased a week later, barely listening to the litany of excuses being offered to him.

"Yes, that's exa—"

"Learn to say more with less, Graeme. That's how this corporation has grown to where it is. Have Sebastyen call me." He ended the call, telling himself to quit acting like every self-important bastard in need of anger management classes he'd ever worked with. He was going on a week without sleep, his appetite shot despite Rowan leaving him hearty stews and tender souvlaki and chocolate brownies that melted on his fingers. He wanted an end to this unbearable tension, but the clock ticking down on his time with her frayed his temper a little more each day.

His laptop burbled with an incoming call. Sebastyen got to the heart of the matter immediately. "We're dragging our feet on several initiatives, waiting on the signing of the petition and the reading of the will. Did you receive the revised documents? Any word on when you'll see forward movement on that?"

Nic glanced at the date on his screen's calendar. He'd been putting off talking to Rowan, knowing it would upset her, but time was running out on that too. He ended the call with Sebastyen and went looking for her.

She was in the breakfast room, where abundant windows around the bottom of the south-eastern turret caught the morning sun and French doors led onto the front court-yard. Bins from the island's thrift store were stacked next to sealed boxes adorned with international courier labels.

"Rowan?"

She jerked, and the look she cast him was startled and wary. They were only speaking when they had to, and every conversation was stiff and awkward. They stared at each other, face-to-face for the first time in days.

Nic wanted to rub at the numb ache that coated his scalp and clung like a mask across his cheeks. His facial muscles felt locked in a scowl. He'd been trying to put her back at a distance, but all he could think was that he'd let her inside him and now there was no way to get her out.

He'd been devastated by her infertility. She wanted a family and something in him desperately wished he could give her one, even though he'd heard her qualifications loud and clear. *The right man. Not now.* His entire being was hollow with the knowledge that even she knew he would ultimately disappoint her.

He took in the growing fretfulness in her eyes.

"What's wrong?" she asked.

"Nothing," he lied, with a pinch on his conscience. "I just need to talk to you about the papers I asked you to sign."

Her back went up immediately. Her knuckles on the pen she clutched glowed like pearls. "I said I'd do it to-morrow. I will."

"That's not it. Legal had to make a change." He took a breath. "After I explained that your parents were still married."

Her brow pleated, but her confused expression quickly gave way to dawning comprehension.

Rowan distantly absorbed what had never occurred to her. The relationship between her parents had been so minimized the last thing she would have called her father was Cassandra's next of kin. *She* was her mother's closest relative. But that wasn't actually true and of course Nic was way ahead of her on that.

"Don't—please don't go to my father with those papers." Waiting to sign the papers tomorrow was her one excuse to stay here with him. For him to yank that away would cause a huge fissure to open in her.

"I was only going to offer to do it if you prefer not to," he assured her gently. "But he does have to be the one who signs."

Her heart gave a hard beat. Of course he did. She should have seen that ages ago. But her mind hadn't been on anything but tomorrow—and not for the reason it should be. She was leaving and her heart was breaking. She shook herself back to reality.

"You caught me off guard. Of course I'll take them to him. I should have realized."

He shrugged off her stilted promise with stiff negligence. They couldn't seem to overcome the intimate revelations of a few days ago. It had drawn a line beneath their relationship, leaving it summed up as unworkable. He wanted children. She couldn't give him any. He thought he was incapable of love. She couldn't prove him wrong when he couldn't love *her*.

Did she love him? Yes. Her girlish crush had deepened and matured into something abiding and strong. But so what? She had thought an affair could bring them closer, that she would touch him, draw him out, but she had turned into yet another person who had raised his expectations and then dashed them. He'd never trust in her love.

"While I have your attention…" she began, and then had to clear her throat.

Her abdomen tightened with foreboding. She told herself to quit being so nervous. It wasn't like she hadn't been mentally preparing herself for this. She had been working nonstop on arrangements, determined to finish by Nic's deadline as a matter of pride. She had talked to Frankie, booked travel, and even begun packing her things. She still found herself beginning to shake.

Get a grip, Ro. You knew the end was coming.

Which was the part that was making her fall apart. Dispensing of things was sad, but they were just things. Even the house was something she was gradually letting go of as she accepted that the people she loved would no longer be there to welcome her into it. There was one thing she couldn't face letting go of, though: Nic.

She tucked a strand from her ponytail behind her ear. Her hand was shaking and she saw his gaze fix on it. She folded her arms.

"I'm almost finished, so I should tell you where everything stands. These boxes are going to a theater manager in London who wants to set up a dedicated display in his lobby. A courier is coming tomorrow." Rowan jerked a look to the ceiling. "Mum's gowns are being auctioned. I gave the auction house your PA's details. They'll set up a convenient time to send a team to inventory and pack those properly."

"You're not keeping any?"

She understood his surprise. He knew as well as she did that designers had lined up to custom-make haute couture for Cassandra O'Brien. They were gorgeous one-of-a-kinds—but they were Cassandra's style, not Rowan's.

"Where would I wear them?" she dismissed. "No, they're works of art, so I'll let them benefit an artist by using the money to set up a trust for my father." She glanced warily at him, bracing against his judgment, hurrying to clarify. "So I won't have to resort to tasteless appearance fees or anything like that again."

If she had hoped for an approval rating she was disappointed. He scowled, seeming both thunderstruck and filled with incomprehension.

"You're not keeping *any* of it?"

It being the collection of her mother's possessions, she assumed.

"Well, a few things, of course." She shrugged, pretending it didn't bother her how judicious—ruthless, even—she'd had to be. The boxes for the thrift store were filled with *chotchkies* that had no value but had been in her life as long as she could remember. She would have kept them for her own home if she had had one. "I kept some snapshots and Mum's hand mirror. The dish she put her jewelry in at night. Things like that."

"What about her jewelry?" He leapt on the word. "Auction?"

Rowan pressed her lips together. "I wanted to ask you about that."

"I'm not going to contest ownership, if that's what you're worried about. Olief would have given those things to Cassandra without any expectation of getting them back. If you want to auction them to give yourself a nest egg, do."

"I don't." She tried to suppress the testiness that edged into her. "I'm not interested in profiting from gifts that marked important occasions in their life. Besides, we won't know if they're mine or my father's until the will is read. I just wanted to ask you to take responsibility. I don't have a safety deposit box or anywhere else secure."

His stare grew inscrutable.

Rowan was hugely sensitive to the air of intensity gathering around Nic like dark clouds—especially because she didn't know how to interpret it.

"I've sorted Olief's things as well," she prattled on. "Just recommendations, of course. He has some gorgeous tuxedos that would fit you with a minimum of tailoring." She couldn't help stealing a swift tallying inventory of his potent physique, turned out professionally for telecommuting in a striped button shirt and tie. "I'd love to include the vintage one with those things going to London if you're okay with that?"

"Rowan, I told you to *take* what you wanted, not…" His jaw worked as he scanned the neatly stacked bins and boxes. "I expected you to identify and keep what amounts to Cassandra's estate—not disperse everything to charity and…" He shot his hand into his pocket where it clenched into a fist.

"I *can't* take much. Where would I store it?"

"But you could sell things for a down payment on a flat and tuition for a degree. Why would you keep yourself as broke as you were when you walked into this house? Are you thinking about your future at *all*? What do you intend to live on?"

She frowned, not liking how defensive he made her feel for a choice she'd already made. It was a risk, yes, but one that actually gave her a sense of excitement.

"Frankie has—"

"Do *not* let Frankie exploit you," Nic said, cutting her off. "I've cleared your debts with him so don't let him bully you. And don't worry about owing me. Forget that. Forget the credit cards from before. I was being a bastard because I was angry. That's in the past. We know each other better now."

"Do we?" He still thought her capable of selling off possessions for rent the way her mother would have. But she was taking a real job—one that was temporary, but paid a weekly wage and would get her on her feet. She was trying to act like an adult while an unrelentingly immature part of her clung to a rose-hued dream that her efforts at showing maturity would raise her in his estimation, that somehow he'd begin seeing her with new eyes. Eyes that warmed with affection.

"I know your love for Olief was genuine, Rowan. I believe he was looking out for you in every way he could because he felt as protective as any father." Nic rubbed the back of his neck. Suffering angled across his face as he added, "I think you helped him become capable of experiencing and showing those sorts of feelings because you draw things out of people in a way I never could. I wouldn't even know how to try."

Tenderness filled her. *You do*, she wanted to insist, because he provoked intense feelings of many kinds in *her*. But her throat was filled with the breath she was holding. Was he saying that she'd taught him to experience deeper feelings than he'd ever expected? She searched his troubled brow.

He tensed his mouth, broodingly. "I'm convinced Olief would have made provision for you and your mother. If he didn't he should have, and I'll honor that. What you had before—accommodation, living expenses—I'll go back to covering them."

Her heart landed jarringly back to earth. Rowan reminded herself to draw a breath before she fainted. It came in like powdered diamonds, crystalline and hard. It took her a moment to find words.

"Let me guess. You'll even let me grace your bed while you pay those expenses?" The bitterness hardening her heart couldn't be disguised in her flat, disillusioned voice.

"That's not how I meant it." His shoulders tensed into a hard angle.

"You're going to pay my expenses and *not* want to sleep with me?" she goaded.

His bleak gaze flicked from hers. "I can't say I don't want you. It would be a lie. The wanting doesn't stop, no matter what I do."

And it made him miserable, she deduced. No mention of love or commitment either.

Rowan told herself not to let his reluctant confession make a difference—especially when he was standing there not even looking at her, his bearing aloof and remote, but her heart veered toward him in hope anyway.

She lifted a helpless palm into the air. "It's constant for me, too, but—"

"Then why can't we continue what we started?" He pivoted his attention to her like a homing device.

"Because I don't want to be your mistress!"

He rocked back on his heels, his jaw flexing like he'd taken a punch.

"I don't want to be *any* man's mistress," she rushed on. "I want a relationship built on equality. Something stable that grows roots. Even if—" Her words were a long walk onto thin ice. She looked down at the pen she had unconsciously unwound so the center of its barrel fell open and parts were dropping out. "Even if it doesn't include children, I still want something with a future."

She looked up, silently begging for a sign that he wanted those things, too.

His eyes darkened to obsidian. His fists were rocks in his pockets.

"You're right, of course," he said, after a long, loaded minute. "All we had was a shelter in a storm, not something that lasts beyond the crisis. I'll never again judge Olief for caving in to physical relief during a low point."

The words impaled Rowan. She nodded jerkily, because

what else could she expect him to say? That he had miraculously developed a deeper appreciation for her place in his life? At best he was nursing a sense of obligation toward her. It was the last sort of debt she wanted to make him feel.

"I'm going for a walk." She needed to say goodbye to Rosedale. It was the final item on her to-do list.

"Stay back from the water."

A bitter laugh threatened, but Rowan swallowed it and left.

Rowan caught a lift with the courier in the morning, giving Nic about three seconds to react to her leaving. She walked into his office, said she could save him a trip to the landing and asked where were those papers that needed signing.

No prolonged goodbye. Just a closed door, the fading hum of an engine, then silence that closed around him like a cell. Her scent lingered in a wisp of almond cookies and sunshine, dissipating and finally undetectable.

Nic stood up in disbelief, drawn to the window where the vehicle had long since motored up the track on the side of the hill and disappeared. He had been girding himself for an awkward leave-taking, expecting something uncomfortable in front of the passengers waiting for the ferry. He had thought they'd have a quiet day today, but he'd been sure she'd spend it here. With him.

His limbs felt numb as a graveled weight settled into his abdomen.

Unconsciously he found himself searching the grounds for her lissom silhouette. But she wasn't at the gazebo, or in the swing under the big oak, nor among the rows of grapevines or even taunting him from the rocky outcropping at the beach. Yesterday he'd watched her wander the estate for hours, often looking back at the house. He'd thought she was waiting to see if he'd join her, but he'd been too disturbed by their discussions in the breakfast room. Too stripped of his armor.

"I don't want to be your mistress."

He hadn't planned any of that: either the offering of a settlement or a continuation of their arrangement. It had come out of the situation as he'd realized she was setting herself up to be destitute. Shame had weighed on him for his arrogance in cutting her off. Rowan wasn't a superficial user. She was too sensitive for her own good, putting other's needs ahead of her own—even people who had deep flaws like her mother and father.

Pushing away from the window, he strode from his office into her room—only to be brought up by the neatly folded sheets on the foot of her stripped bed. He didn't know what he had expected, but it wasn't that.

The night table and dresser top were clear. The closet held only hangers. All the drawers were empty. Even the shower had dried to leave no trace of her. The wastebasket was fresh, the long dark hairs shaken from the floor mat and swept away.

A wild insidious thought occurred that he'd imagined her presence here. The rock music while she had worked, her burbling laugh after a leading remark, the feel of her naked skin against his... His breath turned to powdered glass in his lungs.

She'd given her virginity to him. That meant something, didn't it? She had said she wouldn't forget him, yet...

"Damn you, Rowan!" he squeezed out, instantly needing proof of her existence.

He dragged drawers from their rails and in his impatience tossed their hollow shells to clatter across the hardwood floor. Empty. All empty. With nothing else to throw, he impulsively launched a drawer at the wild-eyed man in the mirror.

His image shattered in a jarring smash that disintegrated into a glinting pile of shards on the floor.

He was losing his rationality, but this was more than a man could bear. He'd dealt with the confusing pain of his father shutting him out and his mother walking away without looking back. He'd even met unflinchingly the gaze of his real father when Olief had looked up from smiling with pride at the girl who wasn't his into the eyes of the man who was.

All of it had devastated him, but this pain was worse.

Driven to the master bedroom, he began overturning boxes. One of them must have photos of her. But they held only Cassandra and Olief, nothing of Rowan. No warmth, no affection, no laughter.

No Rowan.

She had left him.

He'd been abandoned. Again.

CHAPTER TWELVE

Nic's PA blipped into his computer monitor with a message that the auction house was on the phone. He instructed her to tell them to call back next week, not missing the subtle pause before her assent that silently screamed, *Again*?

Pushing back from his desk, he moved to the window, where he rubbed the back of his neck. His whole body hurt from long work days and harder evenings in the gym. Blinking to clear the sting from his eyes, he tried to take in the view of Athens, but nothing penetrated.

He was too aware that if the auction house was calling the week was up for the demolition team, as well. They'd get the same answer, since he couldn't let anyone into the house while it was in the state he'd left it and he couldn't face going back to clean up.

Nicodemus Marcussen, the man who had looked into the wrong end of a rifle twice, not to mention coming face-to-face with a jaguar and surviving a bout of malaria, couldn't find the courage to do a bit of housekeeping and get on with his life. These days he had a lot of compassion for men like Rowan's father, who drowned in alcohol to numb the pain of being alive.

He cursed and hung his head. *Rowan's father.* She wanted to use the auction money to set up a trust for him. Twelve weeks was too long to put that off. Nic couldn't keep doing it. Why hadn't she contacted him to ask what was holding it up?

Heavy-hearted, he suspected he knew. Drawing his hand from his pocket, he examined the key that seemed to end up in his possession every morning. He'd come to associate its rough-smooth shape and metallic smell with guilt, anger and loss, but he couldn't make himself get rid of it. The key or the house.

Rowan expected him to. Everyone did. The architect had delivered the drawings weeks ago. The builders were being put off as well. Nic was sole heir to everything Olief had owned. There'd been provision to support Cassandra and allow her the use of Rosedale, but the house, as part of Marcussen Media, was his. He had every right to knock it down, but he couldn't make himself do it.

Clenching his hand around the biting shape, he recalled the signed documents arriving that had allowed the declaration of death. The Italian painter's signature had been a shaky flourish in all the right places, but there had been nothing from Rowan. No forget-me-not stationery with a snooty missive demanding Nic sort out her finances.

He'd give anything for the privilege, he acknowledged with a wistful ache in his chest, but after a brief game of financial ping-pong with Frankie he'd had to leave Rowan's modest balance for her to pay off. She didn't want anything from him and it hurt so much he couldn't bear it. But what did he intend with a gesture like that?

Connection, he thought simply. He just wanted to know they were still linked in some way. He was becoming as sentimental about attachment as she was.

The spark of irony glinted in his mind, no bigger than a dust mote catching in a beam of sunlight, but he held his breath, examining it.

When had he last felt like this? Truly wanting someone in his life? He'd grown up wanting Olief in his life, but when the opportunity had finally arisen he'd been too tainted by the years of neglect. He'd held back from letting real closeness develop with his father, certain he'd lose in the long run.

And he had.

Everything in him still screamed that it was dangerous to yearn for love and the indelible link of family, but that was what he wanted with Rowan. He'd settle for scraps if he had to, but he couldn't function under the belief that he'd never see her again. He needed to know that his future contained her.

Even if it doesn't include children, I still want something with a future.

How many times had he replayed those words in his head along with his own response that what had passed between them had been only shelter from a storm? He'd been scared when he'd said it. He could offer her a lot of things, including a secure future, but when it came to love he feared his heart was too damaged. *He* was.

He'd thawed a lot under Rowan's warmth, though. It made him think that maybe, if she could be persuaded to keep seeing him…But he was getting ahead of himself. She might not want anything to do with him.

A yawning chasm opened before him as he contemplated going to her and putting his soul on the line. But it wouldn't hurt any more than he was hurting right now. At least he'd know.

And, damn it, he was not a helpless six year old any longer. He was a man who knew how to fight for what he wanted. He would do anything to have her back in his life. To *keep* her in his life.

The decision made him suck in a breath that burned. A

flame of something he barely recognized came to life inside him. Anticipation of relief from pain. *Hope*.

Wherever she'd gone, he'd find her and bring her back to where she belonged!

Rowan watched the little girl appear and disappear between the heavy coats of the bustling street, her face a picture of frightened despair as Ireland's ever-present rain drizzled into it. Her voice, clear and agonizingly uncertain, lifted in a shaky plea. Everything in Rowan wanted to run to her. She was overwhelmed with compassion for this waif who'd lost everything.

Until a man in a modern trenchcoat, his dark blond hair foreign in a sea of black Irish peasant cuts, strode from between the carriages and ruined the scene.

"Cut! What the hell?" someone yelled. "Security!"

"Nic!" Stunned to recognize him, Rowan rushed forward, shock making her stumble. "It's okay, I know him," she assured the men in the red shirts charging forward.

Her whole body trembled in crazed reaction. He looked so good! But tired. His face was lined with weariness, breaking her heart. And he was *annoyed*. He glared at the assistant director when the woman tried to take his arm.

"Come with me, you crazy man." Rowan grasped Nic's wet sleeve and led him away, glancing back at her charge to say, "You're doing great, Milly. I'll be right back."

Little Milly beamed with pride, then stood dutifully still as Makeup approached.

Rowan dragged Nic into a friend's trailer and tried to catch her breath. It was impossible when he filled the space with his dominant presence and masculine scent. Everything about him hit her with fresh power: the authority he projected, the stirring energy he radiated into the air. The sexual excitement he sparked in her with the simple act of falling into her line of vision.

Oh, that physical pull was so much worse now she knew how incredible it was to lie with him. All of her wanted to fall forward and kiss, hold, caress, *be* with him.

She tried to conquer it, tried to quell the shaking and hold on to control. Tried to find her equilibrium and act like a rational human being when he'd just knocked her back after three months of learning to live without him.

"What are you doing here?" she asked with growing defensiveness. "And like that? If someone barged into your board meeting you'd have them arrested."

"Not if it was you." He narrowed his gaze on her mouth. "Why is your accent so strong?"

The sound of his voice, the leading words he'd said, made her heart lurch. She could barely stay on her feet. "Living here does that. And I'm teaching that girl to speak like a native so they won't crucify her for being American. I'm her dialogue coach."

Nic ran a hand across his hair, then dried it on his thigh. "Frankie said you were on a film set in Ireland. I didn't know if that meant you were acting... Can we go somewhere to talk?"

Seriously? She bit down on her lip, shocked by how badly she wanted to go anywhere with him, but self-preservation reminded her to keep her feet on the ground. "We're in the middle of a scene," she pointed out with forced patience.

"Do you like this job?"

His penetrating gaze had an effect that was nothing less than cataclysmic. She had missed those blue eyes, that stern expression, the way he looked at her like he really wanted to hear what she had to say.

"I do. I get to tell people off if I think they're pushing Milly too hard and she's a doll. I'm not sure what will come next. Frankie's looking into an Italian film. But for the moment I have a roof over my head." She tried to make it sound like it was all sunshine and roses, not hinting at how badly she'd been missing him.

"About that… A roof, I mean." He cleared his throat and his hand went into his pocket. "I've done a few things." The mixture of arrogance and sheepishness in his tone made Rowan tense.

"What things?" she asked with low-voiced foreboding.

His hand came out of his pocket and he set a key next to where she was involuntarily clutching the edge of the sink. Recognition hit in stages as she processed the bronze shape, the familiarity of it, the way its sharp angles seemed worn down—and the possessive longing and sense of privilege it inspired only now, after she'd given it up.

"What—?" She couldn't believe he'd come all this way to tell her the house was rubble. That would be too cruel.

"It's yours, Ro."

"Rosedale?" The magnitude of the gift was too much. She had to clap a hand to her mouth to keep her suddenly wobbling chin from falling off. At the same time the tears that filled her eyes stung with loss. She couldn't face that big, empty house without him in it. "I can't," she choked.

"You'd rather I destroy it?" He reached for the key.

She was quicker, snatching it up and holding it in a protective fist against her heart, realizing when she caught the glimmer of smug satisfaction in his eye that he'd been bluffing. He was far quicker than her when he wanted to be.

"Why, Nic? Something in Olief's will?" She couldn't believe it.

He dismissed that with a brief movement of his head. "No, this is my decision. Olief made provision for your mother, but left everything to me. And you must have seen a copy of Cassandra's will by now?"

Rowan hitched her shoulder, dismissing it because it was exactly as she had expected. Gowns and empty purses. Jewelry she didn't want to sell.

"About the gowns—I've had emails," she began with a concerned frown.

"I know. I've…done something else. I went to see your father."

"What?" Dread poured into her, making her want to sink through the floor and disappear. One pained word came out. *"Why?"*

"Cassandra was meant to be taken care of, and he was still married to her. It seemed right to make sure there was something in place for him. Don't look like that, Ro. It wasn't bad. I liked him. I see where you get your sense of humor. And I was there first thing in the morning, so he was relatively sober," he allowed with a diffident shrug. "I've purchased his building, so rent will never be a problem again, and hired a caretaker to go in every day. A man who will cook and clean and has a background in addiction rehabilitation. We had a heart-to-heart, your father and I, about losing parents and that maybe you don't need to face that again any time soon. I don't know if it will make a difference, but…"

"That's incredibly generous, Nic," she said to his shoes. "I'll pay you back—"

He took a firm hold of her jaw, his warm thumb covering her lips to still them as he drew her face up so he could look into her eyes. The impact of his touch, his closeness, the deep eye contact was earth-shattering.

"Don't you dare."

"But—" She was coming apart inside, fighting the urge

to shift her lips into his palm and kiss him. "I don't want to owe you," she whispered.

"You don't want to be my mistress. I know that. None of this comes with a catch. I'm not trying to buy you, Rowan. I just want to know you're looked after, not breaking your leg or—" A completely uncharacteristic agitation seemed to grip him. He took his hand from her face to rub it over his own. "I want to know you'll be at Rosedale sometimes and I might have a shot at seeing you, that you're not out of my life forever."

"You want to see me?" A very fragile hope, one she'd had to tamp down on a million times, began to twine up from the depths of her heart.

He reached into his pocket, drawing out a small velvet box that he set next to the sink with almost confrontational determination. "I want to marry you."

Rowan was so stunned she reflexively backed away until her legs hit the edge of the bench and she sat down in a clumsy heap, her head falling into her hands as she tried to deal with all he was throwing at her. The key dug into her closed fist. Too much to process. Now a *ring*?

"All right, just *see* me," he rushed out gruffly. "That's enough. Just be in my life, Rowan. Even if it's like it used to be—a few times a year. Whatever you want. Just don't make me live with this loneliness that hits every time I think of that house without you in it. I can't go near Rosedale, but I can't knock it down and obliterate the only good memories I have."

"Nic…" Her voice didn't want to work, catching and quavering in her throat while her icy fingers shook against her numb lips. Her heart pounded as though she'd been running for her life and now she was cornered. Not safe, but maybe…just maybe…

"Do you love me?" she risked.

His face tightened and started to close, but before he could withdraw into the unreachable man she could only dream of from afar Rowan threw herself at him, wrapping anxious arms around his rain-dappled coat and big, unyielding body.

"You don't have to say it. This is enough."

"I want to say it," he said tightly, as though struggling with a great burden.

She squeezed him tighter. "It's okay. It's enough that you're here. I love you. I always have." Joy flooded through her as she finally admitted it to herself, to him—

Hard hands caught her upper arms and pushed her away. He held on to her, but his incredulous and furious expression scared her. "You've *always* loved me?"

Oh, she'd made a terrible, horrible miscalculation—opening her heart like this and assuming a bit of nostalgia on his part was anything like the soaring love she felt. Sickened, she could only stand there dumbfounded.

"Then why did you leave me?" he asked in a voice of abject despair.

Shock gave way to a slam of relief, followed by heart-rending regret.

"You can't just rip a man apart like that," he rebuked.

"But you hated me for years. You only asked me to stay as your mistress," she reminded him with a spark of offense. Her pique crumpled as her view of a shared future with him struck a brick wall. "And since I can't give you a baby, and you want one—"

He groaned in a release of frustration and despair, hauling her against him under his wet overcoat and into the shelter of his warmth and strength. "I have been fighting letting you under my skin every second of my life. I knew you'd destroy me if I did, and you have. I hate trying to live without you, Ro. I *need* you in my life. And, yes, I will always wish we could make babies together. But we'll make our family whatever way we need to. If it's only us, that's enough. *I love you*."

His arms crushed her, making it hard to find enough breath to talk, but she wouldn't have it any other way. She was shaking so hard she needed him to hold her up.

"I didn't mean to hurt you. I didn't think I could," she managed.

"You can, Ro. More than you know."

Because he cared. He was letting down his guard for her and she recognized what a sacrifice he was making. She silently swore a vow of duty to protect, never wanting to hurt him again.

His mouth found hers and they kissed with a reverence anointed by salty tears. His hand in her hair was possessive and cherishing, his other hand gently stroking to meld her curves indelibly to his hard angles.

The door to the trailer opened and a male voice cursed. "Get your own room." The door slammed.

Rowan choked on a laugh as they broke apart in surprise, breathless and blinking to see through her wet lashes.

"I've missed this smile," Nic said, with a tender knuckle against the corner of her mouth. "But I agree with whoever that was. What are we going to do? I want to marry you *now*."

"Are you sure?" His urgent determination lifted her heart into the stratosphere, but she forced herself at least to try to be sensible. "We can see how things go—have a long engagement. You and I…we have our clashes."

"We're both too headstrong not to. But I'd rather have a ring on your finger as a promise that we'll work it out."

The deep tenderness in his eyes turned everything in her to liquid heat, but she heard something else in his tone that touched her even more deeply. Implacable determination. He wanted a seal on this deal and no room for her to back out. Nic wanted her. Forever.

With a trembling smile, she held out an equally trembling hand. "Okay, then. Yes, please, I'd love to marry you, Nic. I love you."

He drew in a sharp breath, like he was taking the words into him. His hands shook as he opened the velvet box and worked the ring onto her finger. "I only brought this to prove my intentions were honorable, never expecting you'd actually say yes…"

It was a perfect fit, but the dazzling diamond and its band of emeralds almost made her start crying again. "Not trying to buy me, huh?" she joked, in an effort to hold on to her composure.

"Go big or go home alone." Nic's grin was rueful. He offered her the key to Rosedale.

Rowan tucked it into his breast pocket, giving it a little pat. "You hang on to it. This is a package deal. I don't want the house unless you're in it."

His chest rose as he took a big breath, and they both nearly fell into another passionate embrace.

Rowan made herself check her watch. "Help me show a bit of responsibility here. There's a few hours of filming left. Then we can go back to my flat. It's not much, but I have a feeling you won't be looking at anything but the bedding."

"I won't be looking at anything but *you*."

EPILOGUE

Eight and a half months later...

Nic never closed his door against Rowan, but with workers running table saws and nail guns at the bottom of the stairs while he was trying to work he'd not only closed his door, but started thinking about disappearing to Athens.

Rowan wanted to oversee the renovations, however. If she wouldn't come with him, he wouldn't go. It wasn't his idea to change things, but she was insisting on finding a middle ground between keeping what they both loved about Rosedale while opening up the design more to his preference. Since that would make Rosedale very much *theirs*, he approved.

"Nic?" She pushed in with a confused frown, giving the door a baleful glance as she closed it behind her.

"I couldn't hear myself think with the noise—are you all right?" He was always completely attuned to her moods. Both of them were still capable of putting on a facade around others, but they read each other like a book and Rowan was not herself at this moment.

He scanned her slender figure, stopping where her hands were wringing out the cordless phone like a wet towel. Her face was pale, her eyes wide with shock, her bottom lip caught abusively between sharp white teeth. She was shaking.

Stark concern lifted him onto his feet with instinctive readiness, adrenaline piercing his system like an injection of drugs. "What happened? Who was that?"

"We're in labor," she said, with a sudden beaming smile that instantly became slushy with trembles.

That was supposed to be a joke, he recognized, but his brain wasn't computing humor when the implication was so huge.

"That was the agency?" His knees almost buckled.

If a crowd had rushed in here and hefted him high, touting him as a hero, he wouldn't have been more shocked, elated or proud. Part of him had felt like it was a losing cause to chase adoption. The background interviews hadn't been easy for him. He'd opened up for both of them, to give them this chance, but he couldn't change the fact that he was perceived as a very distant man. The more they'd talked about what they might be able to offer a child, however, the more he'd wanted one. He hadn't been sure he'd even pass muster as a prospective father—now this?

Rowan was nodding and grinning, her brimming eyes spilling happy tears onto her cheekbones. "They have a baby girl. Her mum was killed by a landmine and she was injured. She needs to stay in hospital for a couple of weeks, and will need a number of surgeries over the next few years, but—"

"Us," he said, staggering his way from behind his desk to reach his wife in a lurch. "She needs us."

Rowan nodded, sobbing as she threw her arms around his neck, "Nic, I'm so happy!"

"I didn't think I could be happier than I already was," he choked, lifting and crushing her to him, trying to absorb her lithe frame into his bones. "God, I love you. Look what you're doing to me. Turning me into a father!"

She took his face in her hands and looked at him in the undisguised way that always made his heart bottom out. "You are going to be the most amazing father. I can't wait to see it."

He teared up, and swept her in a scoop against the racing pound of his heart, stumbling to the sofa so he could sit with her in his lap and stroke her shaking body with his shaking hands.

"My whole life is better with you, Rowan. Thank you for loving me."

Rowan was so deeply happy and in love it was more than she could contain. Wiping her damp cheeks, she laughed helplessly, "I can't stop crying and I want to kiss you!"

"Did you have the sense to lock the door?" In one powerful twist he had her gently sprawled beneath him, his weight braced over her. He paused, hand massaging her flat abdomen. "Can we do this in your delicate condition? Being in labor and all?"

She let out a peal of appreciative laughter. "Better hurry before we have a baby stealing our attention."

"When you put it like that, I think I'd better take my time. I want to give you all the attention you deserve." He covered her smile with a reverent, loving kiss.

* * * * *

A sneaky peek at next month...

MODERN™

INTERNATIONAL AFFAIRS, SEDUCTION & PASSION GUARANTEED

My wish list for next month's titles...

In stores from 18th January 2013:

❑ Sold to the Enemy – Sarah Morgan

❑ Bartering Her Innocence – Trish Morey

❑ In the Heat of the Spotlight – Kate Hewitt

❑ Pride After Her Fall – Lucy Ellis

In stores from 1st February 2013:

❑ Uncovering the Silveri Secret – Melanie Milburne

❑ Dealing Her Final Card – Jennie Lucas

❑ No More Sweet Surrender – Caitlin Crews

❑ Living the Charade – Michelle Conder

❑ The Downfall of a Good Girl – Kimberly Lang

Available at WHSmith, Tesco, Asda, Eason, Amazon and Apple

Just can't wait?

Visit us Online
You can buy our books online a month before they hit the shops! **www.millsandboon.co.uk**

0113/01

MILLS & BOON
Book Club

2 Free Books!

Join the Mills & Boon Book Club

Want to read more **Modern**™ books? We're offering you **2 more** absolutely **FREE!**

We'll also treat you to these fabulous extras:

- 🌹 Books up to 2 months ahead of shops

- 🌹 FREE home delivery

- 🌹 Bonus books with our special rewards scheme

- 🌹 Exclusive offers and much more!

Get your free books now!

Visit us Online

Find out more at
www.millsandboon.co.uk/freebookoffer